cop.2

W

Estleman, Loren D
  The hider.

THE HIDER

THE HIDER

LOREN D. ESTLEMAN

DOUBLEDAY & COMPANY, INC.

GARDEN CITY, NEW YORK

1978

All of the characters in this book are fictitious,
and any resemblance to actual persons, living or
dead, is purely coincidental.

Library of Congress Cataloging in Publication Data

Estleman, Loren D
The hider.

I. Title.
PZ4.E815Hi [PS3555.S84] 813'.5'4
ISBN: 0-385-13627-7
Library of Congress Catalog Card Number 77–81786

First Edition

To my brother Charles,
for support long overlooked

THE HIDER

CHAPTER 1

I met him the week we declared war on Spain.

It was the day President McKinley ordered Commodore Dewey to go to the Philippines and take the Spaniards to task for the treacherous and unprovoked sinking of the warship *Maine* in Havana harbor on February 15. The newspapers back east were full of proposed candidates for an elite squad of soldiers, the likes of heavyweight prizefighters Bob Fitzsimmons and James J. Corbett, that would panic the enemy on sight and send them scattering for cover. One suggested that Buffalo Bill Cody take charge of a company of six hundred Sioux Indians and scalp his way to Santiago. It is because of all this excitement that you didn't read in the papers about the spring a youth and an old man struck out across Oregon in search of something that everyone said no longer existed. Nevertheless it happened, and you're reading about it now.

The first time I saw him, he was astride that enormous mule of his, slowly making his way down the steep incline that led past my doorway. Looking back on it, I guess I saw him that way more often than on foot in the short time I knew him. He rode easily, ramrod-straight but loose, letting his free right arm sway with the motion of the mule. It was the biggest mule I had ever seen; it stood a good hand higher than my father's bay, and the upper part of each of its forelegs was as big around as one of my thighs. Of course, I was only eighteen years old at the time, and not as big as I was going to get, but that was still a big animal.

I was pumping water into the wooden trough alongside the porch when I heard him coming, and paused to watch. At first glance, I thought the mule was lop-eared, but as it moved closer I could see that one of its ears had been chewed in half. I say "chewed" because that's what it looked like, all ragged and torn and rimmed with scar tissue, as if some starving predator that was too weak to find anything better had grabbed hold of it and worried it in two. That, together with the rope-thick scars that crisscrossed the beast's muscular flanks, made it a formidable sight.

But it wasn't the mule, big as it was, that first caught my attention. I didn't really appreciate the singular appearance of the animal until I could tear my eyes from the man. He was rail-thin, clad in filthy buckskins and high-topped boots, the toes of which were curled and the soles worn so thin that it must have hurt him to walk over rocky ground. His face, what I could see of it beneath the broad-brimmed campaign hat, was old and bony, and covered with skin the color and texture of his buckskin shirt. There was something about the beak of a nose that would have made me peg him for a preacher if it weren't for his eyes. A preacher's eyes usually look past you, but he had the kind that burn through to the back of your head. I suppose some people, once they have read this piece, will be inclined to put down that fiery glow as a sign of madness, but that wasn't the way it struck me then. It still isn't.

He had a bedroll strapped to the back of his saddle, and, as he drew near, I could see that it was wrapped in a heavy fur cloak of some kind. The scarred butt of a rifle protruded from the saddle's weathered scabbard. Aside from that, he carried no other gun that I could see. That wasn't strange in itself; by that spring of 1898 there were fewer and fewer people in Oregon who packed side arms. The only reason I make note of it is that it just naturally seemed that a man like that would carry a revolver. In the days to come, I was to find out a lot about him that didn't fit.

He didn't speak until he had reined to a halt in front of the watering trough.

"Afternoon." It was a dry, dust-caked voice, straight from the trail.

I didn't reply to the greeting. Actually it was a godawful hot day, the kind that blurs your vision and leaves you bone-tired even if you haven't done anything all day but sit. "The Devil's holiday," Pa used to call it, when he was sober enough to notice the weather. But then, the stranger hadn't said what kind of afternoon it was.

"Something I can do for you, mister?" I said.

"Nothing special." He wasn't looking at me; instead, he passed his eyes around the parched yard, seemingly apprais-ing the place. For a moment I wondered if he were a buyer, and my heart leaped. But his next words brought me back to earth with a thud. "My mule appears thirsty. Wonder if you could spare him a drink."

I shrugged, trying to hide my disappointment. "Why not? As long as you fill it up when he's through. That's the house rule."

"Fair enough." He swung down from the saddle in one quick, easy motion. That surprised me. I had him figured at about fifty-five or sixty years old, and would have expected him to be a lot stiffer. You never can tell where old men are concerned. He was even taller on foot than he appeared while astride the mule. I guessed him to be around six feet or more, which would have made him a giant in just about any town in the West. Somewhere along the line, people have gotten the notion that all westerners back then were tall. This just wasn't true. In all the time I spent on the prairie, which when you add it all up is considerable, I don't think I met five men who were over five foot ten with their high-heeled western boots on. I read somewhere that Pat Garrett was six four, but I don't credit it. You can't believe anything you read these days, un-less it's in the New York *World*. But I'm getting off the track.

I noticed as he adjusted the gear on the mule's broad back that the stranger wore two knives on his belt, both on the right side, and that one was sort of teardrop-shaped, with the narrow part up toward the handle and the curved part point-ing downward. I couldn't see much use in a knife without a point, but I wasn't about to ask him why he wore such a

seemingly worthless item. I was ashamed to show my igno-
rance in those days. Anyway, the other knife seemed right
enough. He took the beast by the bridle and led it to the
trough, where it drank eagerly.

"That sure is a big mule, mister."

He turned toward me and stretched. I thought his arms
would never end. "I reckon so," he grunted. "His pa was the
best cutting horse on the King Ranch."

"Those are mighty fine qualifications," I said appreciatively.
Even as far north as Oregon, stories were told of Richard
King's spread outside of Corpus Christi. It was the biggest
ranch north of the Rio Grande, or at least it had been at one
time. Nobody in those parts had heard much about it in over
ten years. "Yes, sir," I repeated, "that is one big animal. What
do you call him?"

"Mule."

" 'Mule?' Doesn't he have a name?"

He shook his head contemptuously. "Pure foolishness to
give a animal a name. He ain't people. I just call him mule.
He comes when he hears it."

I began to see that there was something more to this
stranger than dust and buckskins.

"Pretty fair plot of ground," he said, running his eyes over
the yard and house once again. I don't know what gave him
that impression. The closest thing that ground had to soil was
a fine yellow dust, pounded into a surface that held more than
a passing resemblance to solid rock. The only life it supported
was an occasional clump of sparse brown grass, and that just
barely. If he'd meant the house, he was even farther off; there
was certainly nothing in that weather-beaten shack that would
inspire an artist, even a bad one. The picket fence, a relic of
my mother's first happy days on the farm, had fallen into a
sad state of repair since her stormy departure nine years before.

I didn't mention any of this. "I suppose so," I lied. "Anyway,
it doesn't matter to me now. It won't be my place much
longer."

The burning embers settled on me. "Bank?"

I shook my head. "No, my pa paid off the mortgage years ago. That was before—" I broke off. Pa's condition after Ma left was none of his business. "I'm hoping to sell it to take care of some debts."

"Your pa's?"

"Yes," I said, before I could think.

"When'd he die?"

I sought not to reply, but the steady glare of those eyes broke me down. "Last month. Consumption." Well, at least I could still lie.

He nodded. As he did so, a little dust worked loose from the brim of his hat and floated to the ground. For a long moment we were silent, and I could hear the mule sucking water from the trough. The stranger had taken his eyes from me and was watching the horizon, as people do sometimes when they can't think of anything to say. But I got the idea he was watching for another reason. I didn't know why, because the horizon was no longer likely to spew up trouble—at least not the kind this man was undoubtedly used to. It was kind of eerie, the two of us not speaking and gazing out over the open land as if we were expecting a great feathered band of heathen Indians to come galloping and hallooing out of nowhere, their tomahawks itching for our scalps. I decided to break the silence.

"Mister," I said, "if you want to fill up your canteen, there's plenty to spare."

He kept his eyes on the horizon. "Thanks."

I reached up and felt the fur cloak that sheltered the bedroll behind the stranger's saddle. It was like thick leather, covered with little clots of coarse hair. It felt like horsehide, but no horse ever had hair like that. I asked him what it was.

He eyed me suspiciously. "How old are you, boy?"

I hadn't expected a reaction like that. "Eighteen," I answered. "Why?"

"That explains it." His eyes softened somewhat. "That there's a buffalo robe, son. I reckon you're too young to know buffalo when you see it."

"Bison," I said, half aloud.

"What?"

"I said, 'bison.' That's the proper name. I learned that when I went to school."

He didn't answer. I had the feeling that he considered my argument beneath notice. I felt very, very young.

The mule stopped drinking and backed up a couple of steps. I focused on this as a means of relieving my discomfort. "How come he stopped?" I asked, incredulously. "The trough's still half full. I never saw a horse or a mule that would stop drinking while there was water left."

"You seen one now, boy." He unstrung the canteen from his saddle horn and dipped it into the water. It made a gurgling sound and filled right up. Tipping it up, he downed a gulp, then filled it to the top and screwed on the cap. "There a town near here?" he asked.

"If you can call it that," I replied. "Just down the road about a mile."

"Has it got a name?"

"Citadel."

"What kind of name is that?"

I explained it to him as best I could. According to what my teacher had told me when I was still in school, a Spanish explorer who had undergone a good deal of grief to get there had named the place *Ciudadelo del Diablo*, or the Devil's Citadel. When a mission was established there twenty years later, however, the Devil was dropped from the name and it became simply Citadel. For some reason this story amused the stranger, because when it was finished he did something that surprised me. He smiled.

It was as if he had just shrugged off the last twenty years of living. He didn't have many teeth, and at least a third of the ones he did have were gold, but the change was miraculous. "The Devil's Citadel, is it?" he said. "I reckon there's a good reason for it being named that."

The smile vanished as quickly as it had come, but while it was there, it added something to his character that I wouldn't have believed existed had it not happened. He removed his hat and passed his sleeve across his forehead. His hair, brushed straight back from his forehead, was as thick as any I'd ever seen, and blinding white. The contrast between that and the walnut-brown of his features was startling. He was like one of those paintings you sometimes see of old westerners painted by young easterners. I was surprised to see that a man like that actually existed.

He replaced the hat, and, with it, his solemnity. "Yeah," he said, more to himself than to me, "I got to pick me up a new pack donkey. Mine pulled up lame two days back. Had to shoot him." He lapsed into silence again. I could tell something was on his mind.

"Boy," he said at last, "I ask this question a lot, and I don't often ask it without causing some kind of stir. All I want from you is a answer, yes or no."

"If I know the answer, mister, I'll do my best to oblige." I was flattered. I had the feeling that I was going to be let in on a rare confidence, and I wondered what it was about me that affected this close-mouthed man in such a fashion.

He scanned the horizon again briefly, then settled his gaze on me. "Have you caught sight of a big brown buffalo hereabouts?"

At first I thought I hadn't heard him right. I gave him my best bewildered expression, but he didn't repeat the question.

"Mister," I said slowly, "the last buffalo in the U.S. was killed over ten years ago."

I thought the statement would anger him, but he didn't blink. "There's one," he said simply.

If anybody else had said this, I would have branded him crazy and ordered him off the property. But if anyone were sane, it was the old man who stood before me. If he weren't, I would seriously have begun to doubt my own state of mind. "What makes you think there's any buffalo left?" I asked. I thought, *We might as well be crazy together*.

"Forty years ago," he said, "there was so many buffalo that all the powder and all the hunters in the world wasn't enough to kill them all. Once in New Mexico I had to stop a supply wagon for twelve hours waiting for one herd to pass; when I woke up the next morning, I could look out and see nothing but brown hides stretching all the way back to the Pinos Altos. Injuns tell me stories of a stampede in Arizona that lasted three days. Well, hunters got thick and buffalo got thin. Each hunt the herds got smaller, till you could count them on your fingers. I killed my last buffalo in '92." He paused, contemplating the horizon. *What was he expecting to see?* "I spent the last six years looking for something to shoot. Drifting all the time. Living off bacon, beans, and the land. Three years ago, I was spending time with a old buddy when he took to his bedroll. Just afore he died, he apologized for holding out on me. Said he seen a buffalo outside Tucson and was on its trail when I caught up to him. He was waiting for me to move on so's he could have it all to hisself. Well, sir, I been chasing that buffalo for three years, going on signs and what people tell me. Arizona. Utah. Nevada. California. And now, Oregon."

I wet my lips. "How can you be sure this buffalo is for real? Maybe some people are having fun with you."

"I wondered about that off and on for three years," he said. "But two months ago, I seen him!"

"You *saw* him?"

"Boy, he was standing on a ridge not sixty yards away from me. I got off a shot, but he was over the ridge and gone. I was close then, but I'm so close now I can smell him."

His last words rang in my ears for several seconds. For some reason I was excited. I'd never seen a buffalo outside of pictures, had never felt any urge to see one in real life, but at that moment I would have given my grandfather's Confederate Army belt buckle for a glimpse of a hoof and a brush tail. My throat was dry, and my heart was thumping like a drum in a parade. "Are you sure he came this way?" I asked breathlessly.

He swung his arm in a direction parallel with the front of the house. "He's been following the same old buffalo trail for months. This one runs right through your spread. He's on his way up to Canada, but he ain't going to make it."

I don't think my brain has ever worked as fast as it did in that moment after he'd finished speaking. Did you ever talk to someone who could make you want the same things he did, even though you knew with one part of your mind that it was impossible? A half hour ago, I would have been satisfied with money in my pocket for Pa's worthless land and a train ticket east. Now nothing would do but that I talk this man whom I had never seen before, and whose name I did not even know, into including me in his plans. I looked around me, taking in the dead farm and the house, looking at what my life would be in the future, thinking of the life I had led so far and comparing it to the one I was likely to lead from here on in, and made my decision. I spoke quickly, lest I get a chance to change my mind.

"Mister, would you care to take along a partner?"

He regarded me for a long moment. What he saw was a tall, skinny kid with nothing to show for eighteen years of living but a gray work shirt, faded blue denim pants, a pair of work shoes, and a Stetson hat that I would never grow into, much less look good in, beneath which stuck out a shock of unruly brown hair. Although I had lived and worked my entire life on the farm, I had no muscles to speak of, and I could pass inspection in Teddy's Rough Riders even if I went a month without shaving. I suddenly became conscious of the fact that I didn't exactly look right for the task he'd be expecting of me. I knew he was going to say no.

"All right," he said decisively. "I can use someone to fetch and carry when I'm played out. But you're going to take care of yourself. I'm too old to learn wet-nursing."

I could hardly believe it. I wanted to shout out loud. But I was proud of the way I controlled myself. "You don't have to worry about me, mister. I've been taking care of myself for a long time."

"You got a horse, boy?"

"My pa's bay is ready to go. I've just got to toss a bedroll on him, is all."

"Then get to it, boy. I got to get supplies and a new pack animal and get back on the trail afore sundown."

I felt like running into the house, but I settled for a fast walk. Inside, I pawed through the debris in a corner of the kitchen and dug out the old woolen blanket Pa used to use when he went hunting. It was riddled with moth holes and it smelled of mildew; it hadn't been used since before Pa fell sick with the liver ailment that killed him, but it was serviceable. I tucked it under my arm and headed for the back door. Spotting Pa's Winchester hanging on the wall, I took it down, unrolled the bedroll, and wrapped the carbine in it. I grabbed my warm canvas jacket and a leather sack full of shells and dropped it into the jacket's deep right pocket. Then I went out to the barn.

The big bay was saddled for a trip into town. Two minutes later, mounted, my gear stowed away behind the saddle, I rode triumphantly around to the front of the house. My new partner was back on his mule when I got there.

"You got a name, boy?" he asked.

"Jeff," I replied. "Jeff Curry."

He grunted. "Jeff's a name for a man. The only Jeff I knowed was a deputy U.S. marshal that got hisself killed in Las Cruces riding through cross fire to give me a seat on his horse. You're going to have to prove you're more than a boy afore I call you Jeff."

"Yessir," I said, automatically slipping into the response I had always given Pa. "What do they call you, mister?"

"Well, I been tagged with a good many names, boy. I wouldn't repeat none of them to my best girl. But you can call me Jack. Jack Butterworth."

CHAPTER 2

If you have ever pulled the stopper out of a sink full of water and trash, and seen what it looks like after the water is gone and the trash has lodged in the drain, then you have a fair idea of what the town of Citadel looked like at the bottom of the Rogue River Basin. I'll never know why the town's founders chose that spot to build. At the end of each rainy season, I half expected to find Citadel beneath sixty feet of water. For some reason, however, it always seemed to make it through the storms intact. I understand a dam has been built in recent years that leaves the whole valley flooded, but I can't say for sure because I haven't been back in a long time. I will say this, though: If such a rumor is true, and the little town I knew is peopled only by fishes and fresh-water clams, it's no loss. A more disreputable collection of misfits I should never hope to see. More about that later.

We reached the town's main street and made for the opposite end, where the livery stable stood perpendicular to the street. As I said before, Jack rode easily, surrendering himself to the mule's swinging gait and letting the animal do all the work. He rode as tall as he stood; astride my bay, I would have had to stand in my stirrups to bring the crown of my Stetson level with the brim of his sweat-stained campaign hat. The conspicuous squeak of my newer saddle added to my feelings of humiliation, but he didn't seem to take any notice of it.

"So this is the Devil's Citadel." They were the first words he had spoken since leaving the house half an hour before.

"This is it," I replied. "It isn't much, is it?"

"I seen less. Virginia City looked like the world's biggest chamber pot a week after the silver mines went dry."

Up close, Citadel didn't look too bad, at that. The street was badly rutted from overloaded wagons rattling back and forth during the rainy season, but it was solid enough now. For the most part, the town was untouched by progress; the false-fronted wooden buildings and weathered boardwalk looked no different from the photographs taken during the 1860s which Henry Stockett had tacked up on the walls of his bank, in which you could barely see the street for all the horses and buggies parked along the hitching rails. But the effect was spoiled when we drew alongside Lloyd Slattery's motorcar sitting with its engine running in front of the little one-story post office. It was a monstrosity of steel and dusty leather, with a gas lantern on each front fender. I thought it looked like a bug. I said as much to Jack.

He glanced at it indifferently. "Seen a man put the butt of a Henry through the windshield of a horseless carriage last year. Owner shot him. Dead. Just couldn't take it, I reckon."

He spoke calmly, with an air of detached interest that reminded me of a schoolteacher. Even so, I got the impression that he would have dearly loved to put the butt of his own rifle through the windshield of this particular vehicle. But he didn't; Jack could take it.

As we advanced, I noticed that we were attracting a considerable amount of attention from the town's inhabitants. Some of them stopped to watch us pass, while others came to the doors of the slopes they were in to get a better look at us. I knew some of them, and I suppose a few others knew me, by sight if not by name. Doubtless they were wondering what I was doing with this old derelict. It occurred to me that many of the townspeople who were much older than I was had never seen a buffalo hunter before, much less a buffalo. The occupation had died out while most of them were still children. I didn't pay any attention to them, and I don't think Jack was even aware of their presence. He was probably used to it.

We dismounted in front of the livery and tied up our mounts to the hitching post nearby. Jack removed the rifle from his saddle boot before going in. It was a fancy piece, with an oversize butt and a barrel to match. The trigger guard, too, was larger than normal size, to accommodate the two triggers that reposed within, one in front of the other. The bore was huge. I had seen its like before, when an acquaintance of Pa's had tried to sell one to him. It was a Sharps buffalo rifle, probably the famed "Big Fifty," or fifty-caliber model, with which hunters had claimed to have brought down game from as much as a thousand yards away. I didn't put any stock in those stories, but it's a fact that, after Pa declined to buy the weapon for fear it was stolen, the acquaintance was hanged in Idaho for shooting a deputy sheriff with it, and that three days later they were still scraping deputy sheriff off the walls of the saloon where it happened. Whatever the gun's qualities, Jack carried it casually, hanging down at his side, but ready to use if he were called upon to do so. I realized then why he never bothered to pack a pistol.

Raul, the boy who looked after the stable in the owner's absence, came out to meet us. Although he was my age, he outweighed me by at least fifty pounds and looked more like twenty. He wore a pair of dirty overalls and nothing else that I could see, other than a worn pair of work shoes. As far as I knew, he was as American as I am, so I never knew where he got a Mexican name like Raul, pronounced Ra-*ul*.

He saw Jack first. "Howdy, mister. Can I help you?" Then he noticed me. "Oh, hello, Jeff." It was sort of a snide, look-down-your-nose greeting, so I didn't bother to acknowledge it.

I said, "Where's Mr. Brooder?"

"He's over at the hotel, eatin' lunch." His attitude toward me didn't improve any. That's the way it always is; the lower your station in life, the more uppity you act toward your betters. I ignored it. When you roll in the mud with a hog, you come out smelling no better than he does.

Jack spoke up. "I need a good pack animal, son. What you got?"

"Pack animal?" Raul scratched his wooly head. I half expected to see a flock of bats come flying out. "Gosh, mister, I
don't know. There ain't much call for them nowadays. Most
folks load up a wagon if they're goin' on a trip. Lloyd Slattery
uses his motorcar."

"Wagons slow you down," said Jack, "and horseless carri-
ages don't last long in the territory I'm planning to cover. You
got a mule or a burro?"

Raul's face it up. "Come with me, mister." He led the way
into the stable. It was dark inside, and much cooler than the
street. In those days I think everyone in Oregon secretly
wished to be a stable hand in the summertime. It was one way
to beat the heat, if you didn't mind working amidst the stench
of sweat and horse manure. Of course, the coolness didn't
seem so inviting when you thought of the Oregon winter, but
then there was usually a potbelly stove glowing red in the
corner and roasting you to a turn, so I guess it was about as
close to the ideal job as the average person was likely to come.
We followed Raul through the fragrant stable until we
reached a stall in the rear of the building. He opened the gate
and went in. A second later he came out, beaming and leading
behind him the sorriest-looking burro I have ever seen. It was
small and spindly-legged, and its ribs showed through its hide
so clearly that you could count them. Some kind of mange
had eaten away the hair around its flanks and shoulders, leaving the skin beneath a raw and pussy mess. A pair of red-
rimmed eyes shone dully from beneath its drooping lids. It
smelled awful.

Raul was grinning from ear to ear. "Some greaser sold it to
Mr. Brooder last year for the price of a meal," he explained.
"Nobody wanted it. We was thinkin' we might have to shoot
it."

To my surprise, Jack didn't say anything. He got down on
one knee and ran his hands over the burro's forelegs, first one,
then the other. Then he did the same thing with the hind
ones. He looked up at Raul. "How much?"

Raul shrugged. "Mr. Brooder paid six bits for it. I reckon a buck's fair."

Jack stood up and reached into his hip pocket. He pulled out a small crumple of dirty bills and peeled one off.

"You aren't going to buy it!" I exclaimed.

"Why not?" said Jack, placing the bill in Raul's dirty palm.

"I wouldn't give two cents for that mangy beast," I said. "Why, he might drop dead before we get outside of town!"

Jack stuffed the rest of the roll back into his pocket. "Boy," he said patiently, "how long can you carry two hundred pounds of beans and bacon?"

I admitted that I wouldn't make it out the door of the mercantile.

"I'm betting that this here burro will carry that much and more for as long as he has to." He took hold of the end of the cotton clothesline that was tied around the animal's neck. "If not, I surely would appreciate your pointing out a better pack animal in town."

I didn't answer. He'd made his point.

He nodded to Raul and we left. After he had tied the burro up beside the mule, Jack said, "I got to pick up some grub. Where can I get the best price?"

"That'd be Slauson's Mercantile, up the street," I answered, pointing out the low, whitewashed building that stood facing the bank. "If you can stand Mr. Slauson's disposition."

"You know him better than me. Maybe you can strike a bargain."

"I won't be going in with you," I said. "I've got some business to attend to before we leave."

"Suit yourself." He stepped up onto the boardwalk and left me standing there.

The two-story red brick building that housed the town newspaper and printing shop served also as the headquarters of J. Bottoms, Attorney at Law. That's what it said on the sign; in reality, I don't think my Uncle Jake Bottoms ever did get around to taking his bar examination. I think this was because he knew he couldn't pass it. He specialized in probate cases, but he spent more time running against Randy Fleet for the office of town sheriff than he did pleading his clients' causes in court. This was because it was a good "graft" position, and nobody had ever known Jacob Bottoms to pass up a chance to line his pockets with shady money. The fact that Pa had drawn up a will four years before he died hadn't surprised me half as much as the news that he had chosen Uncle Jake to be its executor. I'm inclined to believe that Pa was more than a little in his cups the day he wrote out that document, because he hated his brother-in-law and had vowed not to die before he did. An honest attorney would have advised him to go home and sleep it off before he fooled with something as important as a man's last will and testament; but we're talking about my Uncle Jake and not William Jennings Bryan.

I found him in his cramped little office in the northwest corner of the second floor, seated at his desk and reading a newspaper. It was a month-old copy of the New York *Journal*, which he received by the stack once a month by way of stagecoach from Portland. A huge headline across the top of the front page read: "Armed Intervention at Once!" I suppose it had something to do with Cuba. I didn't get a chance to look any closer, because Jake heard me coming and put the paper aside.

He was a huge fat man, weighing right around three hundred pounds, and he had a round bald head that gleamed in the sunlight slanting in through the big west window. He always wore pin-striped suits tailored loose to make him look slimmer, but they only made him resemble an elephant draped in a wagon sheet. He heaved himself to his feet and stuck out a pudgy paw for me to take.

"Hello, Jeff, hello." He had a habit of saying things twice for emphasis. "This is some mess we are getting into with Spain, is it not?"

I ignored the hand and he withdrew it awkwardly. "Some

people might call it a mess," I said testily. "Others might say that we are only defending our life and liberty."

"True, true. Well, what brings you here at this time? It is not yet time for your monthly stipend from your father's trust fund." He indicated that I should take the straight-backed chair in front of the desk and eased himself into his comfortable leather one. The legs groaned beneath his weight.

I remained on my feet. It never pays to get too comfortable when you're discussing business. "I'm here to collect the balance of what Pa left me," I said. "I'm going on a trip, and I'll need it."

He frowned. His gray side whiskers almost touched at the point of his double chin. "This is not according to the terms of the will," he said. "Not according to the terms at all. Your father placed four hundred dollars in my care, from which you are to receive fifteen dollars a month until you turn twenty-one, at which time you will receive the balance. You are not to collect the entire amount until you have reached your majority."

I said, "I won't be twenty-one for two and half years. By then the four hundred dollars will be gone."

"I daresay that your father did not expect to pass away so soon." He spread his hands. "I am sorry, but I am bound by the will and I can do nothing. Nothing," he repeated.

This was lawyer double-talk, and it was getting me nowhere. I decided to appeal to his greed. "If you were to loan me four hundred dollars, the amount to be collected upon my twenty-first birthday," I countered, "you would not be violating the terms of the will, and would set yourself up for a sizable amount of interest."

"It does not seem ethical," he said doubtfully. But I could tell he was intrigued by the prospect. He had forgotten to repeat himself.

"It is perfectly ethical," I answered, "and what's more it is good business. The balance remaining in the trust fund will be my collateral."

"Shall we discuss interest?"

"By all means."

"Shall we say one per cent?"

I frowned. "I was thinking more along the lines of one half."

"One per cent is customary." He had dollar signs in his eyes.

There are those who would think it right for me to remind my mother's brother that we were family, and that blood ties meant more than green paper, but I am ashamed to admit that no such thoughts occurred to me at the time. I have never referred to J. Bottoms as Uncle Jake anywhere but in these pages. He just never seemed like family to me. In all honesty, I don't think it would have made any difference anyway. "One per cent it is," I said.

"One per cent, compounded semiannually," he said.

"Annually."

"Semiannually is customary." He gave me a hurt look, but I stood firm. I had already made one concession, and that was more than my limit. "All right," he said at last. "One per cent of four hundred dollars, compounded annually."

"I would like it in writing," I said.

He got out some paper and wrote out two copies of our agreement. We signed and dated both copies and I put one in my hip pocket. Then he turned in his chair and bent forward to work the combination of the battered black safe that stood with its back to the wall. I should have mentioned earlier that Uncle Jake had decorated his office so that everything of importance (waste basket, safe, file cabinet) was in easy reach of his desk. As fat as he was, I don't allow that he relished the thought of having to get up from his chair for any reason. He counted out four hundred dollars and closed the safe door, but before he gave it to me he favored me with a paternal glance.

"What is this trip you are planning to go on that you need this money to finance it?" he demanded to know.

"I don't think it's any of your business," I replied, and stretched out my palm for the money.

He held it back. "As your only living relative, I have a right to know what you are going to do with the money I am lending you. I have a right to know."

I didn't see any other way out. "I'm planning to journey through Oregon and see the sights," I told him. "I know very little about the state of my birth, and I think it is about time I learned."

"A commendable wish," he said after a moment, and handed me the four hundred dollars. "I have a friend who knows everything there is to know about the north country. If you can wait a few weeks, I will wire him and ask him to serve as your guide."

I paused with my hand on the door handle. "I have already engaged a guide, thank you." Well, it was only partly a lie.

Jack had not yet been waited on when I got to Slauson's Mercantile. Old Man Slauson was behind the counter, handing a sack of flour to Mrs. Fleet, the sheriff's wife. She was a stiff-backed matron in plumed hat and whalebone corset who had been treating Citadel as if it were her town for the past three terms. Jack busied himself in the corner inspecting a display upon which were hung a number of new leather harnesses and bridles. A third man, whom I recognized as one of the local loafers, was leaning against the wall near the counter, his hat tipped back on his head. He munched lazily at the handful of peanuts he had taken from the open sack near his feet.

"Afternoon, Mrs. Fleet," I said politely. "Hello, Mr. Slauson."

He waved me over to the counter. A stout gorilla of a man with a sloping forehead and a pair of hairy forearms that protruded from the rolled ends of his sleeves, he smelled of tobacco and bay rum. "Tell me, Jeff," he whispered, pointing to Jack's broad back, "did you ever see anything as old and dirty as that that didn't crawl out from under a rock?"

A high, nasal snigger coming from the direction of the wall told me that the loafer had overheard him. Jack had, too; out of the corner of my eye, I saw him pause in his fingering of the harnesses and bridles, then resume as if nothing had happened.

I drew myself up to my full height and looked the proprietor in the eye. "Mr. Slauson," I said, "I'll thank you not to make any more such comments about Mr. Butterworth. He is my partner."

"Heavens!" exclaimed Mrs. Fleet, who had been eavesdropping as usual. "He looks like something that belongs in my husband's jail!" This remark brought loud guffaws from both Slauson and the loiterer.

Jack turned around, and, with a flourish, removed his campaign hat and bowed. His white hair tumbled over his forehead. "Mrs. Fleet, is it?" he said softly. "Ma'am, I'd be honored to carry that sack of flour for you."

Mrs. Fleet melted like butter. I could have sworn I saw her blush, but it might have been the poor light in the store. "Oh!" she blustered. "Oh, no, sir. I can manage quite well, thank you." With that, she glided from the store, almost dropping the sack of flour when she stumbled on the threshold. Jack chuckled quietly and put his hat back on.

But Old Man Slauson was not to be put off by the episode. In his youth he had won some acclaim as a bare-knuckles prizefighter, and he still fancied himself a scourge among men. He did a ludicrous imitation of Jack's bow for the benefit of the other man in the store, thrusting his expansive rear into the air and sweeping the floor with his hairy knuckles. "Mrs. Fleet, is it?" he cooed in a tone of syrupy ridicule. "Ma'am, I'd be honored to carry that there sack of flour for yew-w-w."

The other man broke up, and Slauson's bray of a laugh filled the store. Jack didn't pay them any attention as he approached the counter. "I want four sacks of bacon if you got them, and two of beans. Oh, and this." He laid down the six-foot-long strip of leather halter he had taken from the display.

Slauson regarded him sneeringly for a moment. When the

customer said nothing else, he reached beneath the counter and hoisted the required items onto its rough wooden top.

"Better throw in a sack of flour, too," said Jack.

Slauson grunted and crossed to a shelf behind the counter. He had to stand up on tiptoe to reach the flour, and even then he had to reach past a row of sacks of coffee to get to it. The buffalo hunter waited until he had wrestled it onto the counter before he spoke again.

"Coffee too."

The storekeeper gave him a dirty look, but he turned to fill his order. Tiring now, he nearly dropped the heavy package of coffee, but he finally managed to thump it down next to the other items and stood there, puffing and blowing.

"Make that two sacks."

"No, goddamnit!" Slauson took off his white apron and hurled it in a ball to the floor. "Jeff, tell your looney old buddy to pay for his stuff and get out before I bust his face!"

I wanted to say something equally acid, but I held my tongue. Slauson was soft and flabby, but he had been a boxer, and I'd seen what those swollen knuckles of his could do to troublemakers. I didn't want to see that happen to Jack.

Jack didn't show a sign of anger. He just hoisted the enormous Sharps and leaned it on the edge of the counter so that the muzzle tickled the storekeeper's chin. Jack's finger rested on the front trigger. "Another sack of coffee, Mr. Slauson," was all he said.

Slauson's adam's apple bobbed up and down once. The loafer, eyes wide, watched the scene in silence. I reckon he didn't want to do anything that would get his friend's head blown off. Slauson's face was shiny with sweat, and his fat jowls were quivering. And all the time, Jack's index finger kept caressing that big front trigger as if he were itching to pull it. It seemed like ten minutes before anyone spoke again.

"Sure, mister," Slauson said at last. His voice was hoarse. Slowly, lest he make some sudden movement that would startle the man with the gun into firing, he turned to get the coffee.

Jack followed him with the barrel of the Sharps until the second sack was sitting on the counter before him. Then he let the butt slide to the floor. The storekeeper's breath came out in a wheeze. "Thank you kindly, Mr. Slauson," he said cheerfully. "What do I owe you?"

He told him.

Jack reached for his pocket, but I stopped him. "I'll pay for this, Jack." I pulled the money Uncle Jake had given me from my hip pocket and peeled off the amount quoted by Slauson. Jack didn't argue. I paid the pale storekeeper, lifted my share of the supplies onto my shoulder, and went out the door. Jack was right behind me, carrying a sack of bacon and two sacks of beans.

"Afternoon, Mr. Slauson," I heard him say.

CHAPTER 3

"Jeff! Jeff Curry!"

I recognized the voice as soon as I heard it. Everybody in town was familiar with Esther Corcoran's throaty rasp. I turned and there she was, all ninety-five or so pounds of her, standing on the threshold of the post office and waving so hard it looked as if her arm were going to fall off. I looked to Jack to see if it was all right to join her.

He was busy securing the bundles on the burro's flea-bitten back. "I'll take care of this, boy," he said. "Go tend to your business."

I thanked him and stepped up onto the boardwalk. Mrs. Corcoran met me at the post office door. She had been Citadel's postmistress for as long as I could remember. Her first husband, a man named Adams, had taken her west from her home town of Philadelphia after the Civil War, but they had only gotten as far as Wichita when Apaches attacked their wagon train and Mr. Adams was killed. She was wounded in the fight; old-timers swore that an arrow had passed straight through her voice box and pinned her to the top bow of her wagon, leaving her incapable of speaking above a whisper for the rest of her life. The story may be an exaggeration, but it is true that she wore high lace collars ever after to hide the scar. While recuperating in Wichita, she met and was taken with a young express-office clerk, Francis Corcoran by name, and a year later they were married. If you look up Oregon in the W. P. A. Writers' Project, you'll see Francis Corcoran credited with the establishment of the first U. S. Post Office in Jackson

County. He died of pneumonia in the winter of 1886, and that was when Mrs. Corcoran assumed the role of postmistress, which she was to hold until she passed away at the age of sixty-eight just when the United States was getting set to enter the World War.

"Did you want me, Mrs. Corcoran?" I said, removing my hat.

She smiled at me and nodded. To do so, she had to tip her head away back, because there was a distance of about a foot and a half between the top of her head and mine. "A letter came for you yesterday," she croaked. "I was just thinking about sending someone out to deliver it when I saw you in the street." She motioned for me to follow her, and tottered back inside the building. I should mention here that, although Mrs. Corcoran was not yet fifty years old, in looks and actions she was just like a woman of seventy. I suspect that her ordeal at the hands of the savages in Kansas had something to do with this.

The post office occupied only a quarter of the one-story frame building; Mrs. Corcoran and her daughter had living quarters in back, and Zeke Donaghue rented the space on the other side of the partition for his harness shop. This left just about enough room for a man of medium size to walk between the heavy oak counter from behind which the postmistress conducted her business and the wall. If someone built like my Uncle Jake wanted his mail, he had to ask for it through the caged window in front of the building. I waited in front of the counter while Mrs. Corcoran scanned the pigeonholes that lined the far wall in search of my letter.

"Dear!" she said, half to herself. "When will I ever learn to put things where they belong? I know I had it this morning. Theodora! Come help me look for Jeff's letter!" She called this last in the direction of the living space in back.

I sighed. Out in the street, Jack had finished loading the burro and was removing the cotton clothesline from its neck in preparation for replacing it with the leather halter he had bought at Slauson's. "I'm in kind of a hurry, Mrs. Corcoran," I prodded.

"Theodora!" she rasped. "Where is that girl?"

I heard a footstep at the far end of the building. I was beginning to get suspicious. "Mrs. Corcoran, do you really have a letter for me, or are you just trying to fix me up with your daughter again?"

She went on rummaging through the stacks of mail as if she hadn't heard me. She had a peculiar kind of deafness that only showed up when something was said that she didn't want to hear.

"Yes, Mama?" Theodora Corcoran came in from the back, her skirts swishing against the bare plank floor. I suppose she was considered pretty for those times, but then so were a lot of girls who would not get past the gate at a beauty contest today. Anyway, she looked better than most. She had that kind of hair that looked black when she was indoors, but which glowed red the minute she stepped outside into the sunlight. She had been popular in school. I guess she was about a year younger than I was.

"Oh, there you are, dear," said Mrs. Corcoran, as if she hadn't known her daughter was back there all the time. "Do you know what I did with Jeff's letter that came in yesterday?"

"No, Mama, I haven't seen it."

Her mother adjusted her gold-rimmed spectacles on her nose and peered as through a spyglass into each of the holes in the top row of the varnished wooden case. "I just can't seem to find it," she said in her whispery voice. "Do you suppose I'm getting feeble-minded?"

Theodora chose to be tactfully silent.

"Look through those sacks, will you, dear?" Mrs. Corcoran indicated the canvas sacks with "U.S. MAIL" stamped on them sitting in the corner behind the counter. "Maybe Jeff can help you look."

"I don't think that's allowed, Mama. Jeff isn't employed by the federal government."

"Well, what difference does that make? Neither are you."

An apprehensive glance passed between Theodora and me. I shrugged surrender and came around the end of the counter to help her search.

"Is there a letter?" I whispered, holding open one of the sacks while she sorted through the mail inside.

She shook her head. "I don't know. Mama mentioned it yesterday, but you can never tell with her."

We searched in silence for some minutes. Then she said, "I didn't see you at the dance last Saturday night."

"That's because I wasn't there," I replied. "Olaf Peterson's cattle broke through the fence onto my property and he and I were all night chasing them back. I slept straight through church Sunday morning."

"Are you going somewhere?" she said, after another pause. "I saw you coming out of Slauson's with that old man."

"His name is Jack Butterworth, and he knows the West like the surface of his saddle. We're taking a trip through Oregon."

"How long will you be gone?"

"As long as it takes to see all the sights," I said. "Quite a while."

"Will you be back in time for the Memorial Day dance?"

She'd said it quickly, and most of it went into the sack of mail, so that I wasn't sure I'd heard her right. I tried to look at her, but she kept her attention on her work. I said, "I'll try."

"Well, I certainly can't find it." Mrs. Corcoran gave up on the pigeonholes and came over to us. "How are you children doing?"

Theodora rose and nodded for me to close the sack. "It's not here, Mama," she said. "We looked through everything."

Her mother made a little sound of exasperation. "I'm sorry, Jeff," she said. "All I can say is that we'll try to have it for you the next time you come to town."

"That might not be for a long time. I'm going away in a few minutes." I said good-bye and strode around the counter. Mrs. Corcoran followed me and stopped me at the door. A little line of worry showed on her forehead.

"Why can't I get you two together?" she said.

"I don't know, Mrs. Corcoran." I shrugged. "Maybe I'm not Theodora's type."

I stepped out the door and rejoined Jack. He was seated on his mule. He had looped the new halter around the little burro's neck and tied the other end to the horn of his saddle.

"All set, boy?" he asked.

I mounted the bay. "All set."

"Then let's ride. Daylight's a sometime thing." He gave his mule a kick, and we started back the way we'd come.

The sun was on the decline when we got back to the extinct buffalo trail. To the north, the horizon was obscured beneath a row of metallic gray clouds which brought with them a breath of sharp, wet air and the promise of rain. It didn't seem like the best time to be embarking on a long trip, but I didn't mention this to my partner. After three years, I figured he'd know more about that sort of thing than I would in ten. I sneaked a long, hard look at the house as we went past it. From this angle I could see nothing about the lopsided farmhouse and the remnants of the picket fence that could have held me there for eighteen years. It had been home, but now it was just another of those prairie hovels through the fissures of which the wind whistled in and out as it does through the mouth of an abandoned mine shaft. I kicked the bay and trotted up to Jack's side without another glance back. I felt free.

"He's been through here in the last couple of days," said Jack. "We're hot after him now."

"How can you tell?" I asked.

"Little things. Broken grass. Turned earth. See that tree, with the bark all rubbed off one side? He does that to sharpen his horns. Yesterday I seen some droppings. We're right behind him, all right."

We spent the remainder of the day following a path which time and climate had rendered almost invisible. Once, great herds of the brown giants had tramped through this area on their migratory path to Canada, but now it was all grown over and planted with wheat and corn so that Bill Cody himself would have had trouble tracking the one that remained. But if tracking was difficult, Jack didn't say so. He covered every inch of ground with his eyes, missing no detail and making no comment except to point out an obscure sign here and there. The trail—what there was of it—kept more or less parallel with the Rogue River, now bearing close to its grassy bank, now meandering away until the raging torrent shrank to a glistening thread in the distance. Along about sundown, we came to a point where our quarry's path was crossed by a gate in a log fence, from where it continued across a farmer's field. I was curious as to how such an ungainly beast had managed to leap a four-rail fence, and asked Jack about it.

"Don't never sell them short, boy," he said. "Once I seen a old bull leap a twelve-foot stream in the Texas Panhandle just when me and Charlie Jones thought we had him cornered. There ain't nothing they can't do if they want to bad enough."

"But why would he want to jump here?"

He shrugged, a rapid up-and-down movement of his lean right shoulder. "Any number of things. Seeing as how he's the last of his kind, I reckon he's more than a mite skittish where humans is concerned. Could be he caught some farmer's scent and took the quickest way out."

Jack dismounted and pulled out three of the logs to let me through on horseback, then led his mule and the burro across. He had bent to replace the logs when a man on the back of a stout work horse came galloping over the hill and reined in facing us. The horse was a cobweb gray in color, and still wore its blinders. "You, there!" he challenged. "Who are you and what're you doin' on my land?" He was a blunt-featured farmer in bib overalls and a gray flannel work shirt, and he had a double-barreled shotgun pointed at Jack with its barrels resting on his left forearm. He was hatless and his brown hair was beginning to thin in front. I recognized him instantly.

"Hello, Mr. Bullock," I said, friendly-like. This caught him off guard, and he squinted against the sinking sun to get a look at my face.

"Who's talkin'?" he demanded.

"Jeff Curry, Mr. Bullock. We met last year when Pa and I brought our sow to your place and mated her to that big old razorback you used to have. Remember?"

"What's your pa's name, son?" His tone had lost some of its edge.

"Frank. Franklin Curry. He named me Jefferson."

"Frank *Curry*?" The hand holding the shotgun relaxed and the barrels drooped about two inches. "Hell, in the old days me and Frank Curry pulled the cork on more jugs than the *en*tire Grand Army of the Republic! You're his boy?"

"Yes, sir."

"Well, it sure is a small world. Who's this you got with you?"

I introduced them. Jack touched his hat with his thumb and forefinger as a sign of greeting.

Bullock acknowledged the gesture with a nod. "Sorry about pullin' down on you like that, mister," he said. "I got to be careful. For all I knowed, you was another jasper tryin' to ride through my cornfield."

Jack perked up at that. "It happened before?" he prompted.

"Son of a bitch galloped right through this same area last week. Tore hell out of my crop over on the south forty. It was only pig corn, but it cost good money and time to plant it."

"You see it happen?"

He shook his head. "Nope, my boy Bob was comin' home cross-lots from school when he heard hoofs thumpin' ground and the top log in the gate come down with a thud. Says he could hear it crashin' through the corn for five minutes."

"What day was this?" said Jack. His voice was calm, but I could tell he was burning up inside. So was I.

The farmer frowned, trying to think. "Let's see; it was the day I finished plowin' the north forty for the later corn. Friday, I reckon. No, Saturday."

"Was it Saturday?" This time I caught an impatient edge in Jack's tone.

"It was Saturday."

There was a pause while Jack digested this information. Then: "You know where he come out?"

"Do I! The son of a bitch took out ten yards of good barbed wire along my western property line. Only consolation I got's his horse will never win no beauty contest. We found enough hide stickin' to that fence to build a whole new animal."

"You suppose me and the boy could take a look at that spot? This sort of thing interests us."

Bullock said, "Why not?" and swung his horse around to take us to the spot.

The path through the cornfield was nine feet wide. We crunched over the broken-down stalks of early corn for a hundred yards or so until we came to the fence, where Jack and I dismounted. The farmer remained astride his horse.

"We just about got her fixed now. That there's some of what he took out." Most of the fence had been replaced, but he pointed to a tangled mess of rusted barbed wire piled at the foot of a big maple tree on the edge of the cornfield. Jack reached down and detached a tuft of something from one of the barbs.

"That's some of the hide," explained Bullock unnecessarily. "Funny kind of stuff, ain't it? Don't look like no horse I ever seen."

Jack handed me the tuft. It was just like the hair on the robe he kept tied over his bedroll.

After swapping some comments with the farmer about the weather and other unimportant things, we said our farewells and passed through the gap in the fence back onto the trail. We found some brown spots that Jack said was blood, but I can't swear to it because it was hard to see them against the scarcely lighter brown of the bunch grass. By this time the sun had slipped below the horizon; many experienced trackers would have given up for the night, but we rode on, Jack using the faint traces of light that remained to follow a trail that only he could see. It grew so dark that I could barely see the reins in my hand, let alone the trail ahead, but still we traveled. We were ten miles north of Bullock's farm when at last I heard him dismount.

I followed his lead. My foot brushed a small shrub and I tied the bay to it. Jack tethered the burro to a blackberry bush, but his mule had been trained to stop when its reins touched the ground, so he left it alone. A half-moon had appeared from behind the creeping cloud bank to cast a dirty gray light over the surrounding hills. As my eyes became accustomed to it, I could see Jack loosing a sack of bacon from the burro.

"I'll get some firewood," I volunteered.

Jack grunted a reply of some kind, and I trudged off toward the wooded area to the east.

When I returned a few minutes later with an armload of wood, Jack already had a fire going from kindling he'd picked up around the area. I was anxious to heap more wood onto the fire and get it crackling—the night air was getting nippy —and I guess I went too fast, because the next thing I knew the flames had gone out and a little wisp of smoke escaped the heap like a sigh. I braced myself. I expected Jack to sail into me like Pa used to when I did something foolish, but he didn't. He just took out another of the matches he kept wrapped in oilcloth in his saddlebags and rekindled the fire.

Two or three minutes later, he said, "Fire's a thing you got to be careful with. It can mean your life up in the snow country, where it gets to forty below after sundown in December." He reached into the open saddlebag and pulled out a cast-iron skillet about eight inches in diameter. With his conventional knife he began slicing strips of bacon to lay in the pan.

"I'm sorry, Jack," I said.

"Don't be. Just don't let it happen up in them mountains, unless you like raw fish. I et some once in Colorado. Can't say as I particularly cared for it." His task with the knife completed, he placed the skillet atop the fire. Within a few seconds the bacon began to sizzle. The smell reminded me that I hadn't eaten since breakfast.

He looked up and saw me watching the bacon. "Hungry?"
I said, "I'm starving."

He grunted. "Closest I ever come to starving was in Texas
in '68. That was the year me and Charlie Jones cornered that
old bull I told you about near Amarillo." He used the point of
his knife to slide the bacon around in the pan and grease the
surface. The frying strips hissed and spat hot grease onto his
cheeks and forehead, but he appeared not to notice it. "It was
three weeks after we split up," he recalled. "A mountain lion
mauled a little girl to death outside of Sierra Blanca and took
off limping for the high country with a double load of
buckshot in its right hip. Sheriff put out a two-hundred-dollar
bounty on its hide. I carried a Spencer repeating rifle in them
days; I took it and a little black-and-white burro I brung from
Nogales and tracked that cat clear into the Quitman Mountains. I was six days out and six thousand feet up when I lost
my burro. Just dropped clean out of sight, along with all my
grub and ammunition. That left me with just the Spencer.

"There weren't no sense in going back; it was mountain
behind me and mountain up ahead, so I slung the rifle over
my shoulder and headed on up the grade." Manipulating his
knife like a spatula, he slid the blade beneath the strips of
bacon and deftly flipped them over. "Game was scarce, it
being winter," he continued. "Even if it wasn't, I didn't think
it right to waste the cartridges I had in the gun on anything
but mountain lion. The next day I was hungry enough to eat
the business end of a skunk. Four days later I had to use both
hands to put my hat back on after it fell off. By the end of the
week I could feel my belly brush my backbone every time I
sucked in.

"To make things worse, the grade got steeper and steeper
until I had to grab ahold of the slippery rocks and pull myself
up an inch at a time. All the time I kept thinking about all the
steaks and potatoes swimming in dark brown gravy I would
buy with that two hundred dollars. I reckon I was more than
a mite crazy by that time. Two weeks out of Sierra Blanca, my
hands bloody and my belly full of grass and nettles, I clumb

up onto a rock shelf and fagged out with my legs hanging over the edge.

"I woke up with a ripping sound in my ears. At first I didn't know where I was, but then I felt that hard rock under my chest and I remembered. I rubbed my eyes to clear out the sleep. And then I saw him. That ripping sound I heard was a growl, and it was coming from the throat of a mountain lion standing not fifteen feet from where I was laying with my legs dangling over the side of the ledge."

The bacon was almost done, but I no longer cared. I hung on Jack's words.

"They always told me that everything grows big in Texas," he went on, "but I never put any store in it up to that moment. That cat must of stood eight hands high at the shoulder, and I reckon it would of dressed out to right around a hundred and eighty pounds if it ever got any meat on its bones. I could count its ribs from where I laid; there was twenty, ten on each side. It had come down from its lair near the peak of the mountain and stopped when it seen me. Its right hip was black with blood and its ears drooped, but when it seen I was awake it hunkered down and got ready to spring. I reckon it was as desperate for food as I was.

"Slow, because I knowed that any quick moves on my part would startle that cat into pouncing, I worked my left hand around to my right shoulder and slipped it under the buckhide sling. This weren't no easy job, remember; I was about as near dead from starvation as a body can get and still be moving around. After about a hundred years I freed that rifle from my shoulder and sweated to get it under my arm without dropping it. And all the time that cat's eyes was watching me, all yellow and filmy. Just waiting for me to make a wrong move. My fingers was so torn from the climb up that I could scarce feel the rifle in my hands, and I had to fumble a mite afore I found the trigger. All of a sudden I lost my grip. The action come up against the edge of the rock with a bang and that cat sprung.

"Its snarly roar echoed up and down the mountain. I seen a

flash of white as its belly shot over my head, and then I stuck
the barrel of the Spencer straight up and pulled the trigger. I
don't think I ever heard no more welcome sound than the
baroom of that rifle going off and the sound of that cat's guts
splatting all over the rock wall behind it. The lion come down
on my shoulder like a ton of bricks and I near fell, but then it
glanced off and went tumbling into open space. I found its
carcass at the bottom of the mountain. I et mountain lion all
the way back to Sierra Blanca."

At the end of his story, Jack removed the skillet from the
little campfire and tossed the strips of bacon into a pair of tin
plates he had taken from his gear. We ate in silence for some
minutes, Jack using his knife while I made use of the ancient
utensils he carried and washed it down with water from my
tin cup. I was the first to break the peace.

"Jack," I said, staring into my cup, "what are you going to
do with that buffalo after you find it?"

"Shoot it," he said. He swabbed a bit of bacon around in his
plate to clean up the grease.

"No, I mean after that."

He stopped eating. "I don't know. I ain't give it much
thought. Reckon I'll take the hide and leave the rest for the
wolves and buzzards."

"Seems like an awful waste."

"Well, how about this?" He put his plate to one side and
wiped his greasy fingers on his shirt. "Me and you, we'll build
us a bonfire and eat buffalo steaks for a week. The rest we'll
make into jerky and split it up between us to have on the trail.
That way we'll be paying the critter the respect he deserves,
and appease our hunger at the same time. Ever eat hump
steak?"

I shook my head.

"Well, you're in for a treat." He got to his feet and went
over to check our mounts.

It was the work of twenty minutes to wash the dishes and
get the camp ready for bed. Jack had only to spread out his
soft buffalo robe on the ground to make himself a comfortable

berth, but I was able to create something almost as good by bunching grass and last year's fallen maple leaves into a makeshift mattress near the fire. I didn't realize how completely exhausted I was until I crawled under Pa's old blanket and settled my aching muscles into the soft natural cushion. I had no trouble getting to sleep. My dreams were of buffaloes and mountain lions.

CHAPTER 4

There was no dawn next morning, just a slight lightening of the sky to the east. During the night the bank of clouds I had taken the measure of the day before had rolled in to create a great dark ceiling that blotted out the blue of the sky and cast its gloomy shadow over everything. The air was raw.

"Wet weather coming," warned Jack, in the midst of saddling his mule. As if to confirm his statement, a rumbling peal of thunder uncurled itself over our heads like a mule skinner's whip. I was thinking that our wisest course lay in making for shelter as soon as possible, but Jack explained that you could tell how close a storm was by counting the seconds between the lightning flash and the thunder, and that we had plenty of time, as there was almost a full minute between them. I reckon somebody up there didn't know this piece of useful information, though, because we had made less than a hundred yards on the trail when the clouds opened up and dumped about three hundred gallons of water over our heads in the first minute.

There wasn't a house or even a lean-to for miles around. Well, there was Bullock's place ten miles back, but getting Jack to double back on a "hot" trail was like inducing a dog to stand still while you bobbed its tail. I gave up after a couple of tries and huddled my chin into the collar of my canvas jacket while Pa's bay, as game as ever, splashed forward through the soupy mud without so much as a whinny of complaint. I'll say this for my partner, though; anytime he wanted to, he could have taken that buffalo robe from behind his saddle and draped it around himself and it would have shed that rain like a slicker, but he knew I had nothing for my own protection, so he left it where it was. Some of you might say, well, if he was so considerate why didn't he give the robe to me? The answer is that he was too considerate to risk insulting me by offering me something he had disdained for himself. That's what a partnership is all about; when one suffers, you both suffer, and if that arrangement doesn't appeal to you then you had best go it alone, because no one is going to want to accompany you.

Jack said he knew of an abandoned building west of Quartz Mountain that had once served as a line shack on a cattle range owned by someone named Ford Harper, but that to get there we had first to cross the South Umpqua River and then follow along its right bank for another five miles through the driving rain.

I said, "Sure, why not? We can't get any wetter than we already are," and so we swung east toward a fording place Jack remembered from his scouting days during the Indian wars.

The only thing wrong with this plan is that when we got to the place Jack remembered, he wasn't sure that that was the place at all. It had been a lot of years, he explained, and with the rain coming down in sheets and chopping the water into a muddy mess it was hard to tell just how deep it was. He added that even if this were the right place, there was no guarantee that the river had not undergone a change and that the only safe spot to cross was not now several miles downstream. We were in a pretty fix.

"One thing's sure," he said, shouting to be heard above the downpour that streamed off the brim of his hat and drenched his buckskins; "We won't never know if this is the right place unless we give it a try." So saying, he twisted the leather halter by which the little burro was secured to his saddle horn around his left wrist, kicked his mule, and all three plunged forward into the swelling torrent.

The mule floundered a little, and for a moment it looked as if Jack, his mule, and the burro were going to be swept along in the powerful current. I had a vision of myself continuing alone on the hunt. But after much splashing and kicking, the huge beast found a footing and thrashed across to the opposite bank, its pygmy cousin swimming along in its wake. Once on solid ground, the mule stopped and shook itself mightily.

Now it was my turn. Jack swung about and raised his long left arm in a beckoning gesture. I took a deep breath. Well, it was only water. Shrugging, I slapped my bay hard on its rump and we hit the river at a gallop. The water thrown up by the churning of my horse's powerful forelegs lashed me in the face, burning my nose and blurring my eyesight. I could feel the current surging past the calves of my legs, could feel it trying to sweep the bay off its feet. I leaned forward and hugged its great neck in both arms. A second later we had cleared the water and were treading on muddy ground, slippery but solid.

I admit that I was feeling pretty cocky. I'd crossed water before, but the rivers that ran through my property were creeks compared to the Umpqua. As far as I knew nobody had ever attempted to ford the Rogue River. Jack brought me down to earth fast.

"If you liked that, wait till we get to the North Umpqua," he said. "It's twice as wide and near three times as fast."

If the sun had ever had the nerve to show itself on that wet day, I suppose it would have been past its high point by the time we finally drew within sight of the line shack Jack had mentioned when we were still south of the river. I can't say it wasn't a welcome sight after all those hours of riding through the pouring rain, but I did wonder if it was worth all the effort. From the outside it was a little square building with a roof full of curled shingles and weeds up to the windowsills, only one of which had any glass in it, and that a single unbroken pane discolored with age and grime. I was glad to see a rusty stovepipe sticking up from the roof, for that meant a stove, but I wasn't too happy to note that the front door was missing. Judging by the shack's run-down appearance, I concluded that it had been quite a while since Ford Harper had controlled his ranch with a firm hand, if indeed the ranch still existed, which I doubted.

There was no stable, but a sort of pole barn had been constructed behind the shack which made use of five or six poplar trunks to support a roof of corrugated iron, the high side of which was nailed to the roof of the building itself. Although it sagged some on one side, Jack counted it sturdy enough to trust our mounts to its shelter. We used our saddle blankets to rub the animals down as best we could, including the burro, and then we covered Jack's mule and my horse with a pair of musty blankets I had found inside the shack. We figured the burro could wedge himself in between the others to keep warm. Then we went inside.

It wasn't too bad, if you didn't mind rats' nests in every corner and the smell of mildew. There was even a rickety table with four chairs around it and a bed; the last was a homemade wooden boxlike contraption with one broken leg and a rotted straw mattress from which the rats had taken the material to build their nests. I grabbed a broom I found in a corner and set to work sweeping the nests and other assorted trash out the door. I would have swept the floor, too, but that didn't seem to make much sense since there wasn't any. One of the nests turned out to be occupied. I jumped about two feet when a big gray old grandfather rat scurried out and ran over the toe of my shoe. I helped him out the door with a hearty kick that made him squeal when he hit the ground.

Jack got a fire going in the little two-burner stove with straw from the mattress and fed it with wood that had been in the box beside it for neither of us knew how many years; with that, and with his buffalo robe hanging over the entrance in place of the missing door, the place lost a good deal of its gloom. I got out of my wet clothes and draped them over a chair in front of the stove. Then, wrapping myself in Pa's old blanket, I huddled up as close as I could get to the stove without burning myself and sat down on the floor with my back against the wall. I asked Jack if he weren't going to do something similar.

"Nope." He leaned on another chair, wobbled it to test its sturdiness, then swung it into position beside the one my clothes were drying on and sat down. I heard his buckskins rustle wetly as he stretched out his long legs toward the source of heat. "When you're wearing hides and they get wet, you got to leave them on till they're dry, else you'll never get back into them. Nothing shrinks like wet skins."

"You'll catch your death of cold," I said.

He scowled. With his damp white hair plastered back and hanging down past his collar, the expression made him look like an old Indian chief. I wondered idly if he had any redskin in his background. "Ain't never got sick yet," he said. "Onliest time I was ever in bed past six was the day a twelve-pounder slipped its chocks at Antietam and rolled over my left leg. I was back on the field the next morning, and I brung three Yanks to ground afore a ball from a Colt Dragoon snapped my crutch in half and sent me back to the hospital to get my leg reset."

I said, "I didn't know you were in the war."

"I brung fifteen men with me from the gold camp in Columbia." His voice was solemn. "They made me a captain. Three years later I was the only one left."

"What did you do after the war?"

"Well, after three years on the losing side, I figured it was time to hitch up with some winners, so I went down to Mexico. Revolution was going full tilt by then. I seen some action outside of Durango, but it got over fast and I come back north. That's when I picked up that little burro that took a sail off the Quitman Mountains."

"What side were you on down there?" I asked.

A tired form of the grin I had first seen in front of my house flickered over Jack's cracked and pleated lips. "The wrong one," he said simply.

He was in a storytelling mood. I took advantage of it. "Jack," I said, "what made you take up hunting buffalo?"

Again he smiled, faintly and with a trace of weariness. "We didn't much call it hunting back then," he corrected. "There was so many you didn't have to hunt. We called ourselves hiders. I don't know why I took it up. I reckon it was just something to do."

"I guess there were a lot of things to do back then," I prompted.

"Yeah. I reckon there was."

He had grown very quiet suddenly; I think I had found what it was that seemed to trouble him so, and I encouraged him to talk about it. "Things aren't like that any more, are they?" I said. "There's not much chance for a man to prove himself now, is there?"

"There's some things," he said. He was staring at a crack in the base of the little stove through which the flames showed. Rain roared on the roof and splattered into the dusty old preserve jars we had found and paced under the numerous leaks. "There's trouble brewing in Cuba. I reckon there'll be plenty of ways for a man to prove hisself once them guns start rolling."

"It isn't the same."

"No," he agreed. "It ain't the same. They say it's pretty, with all the brass bands and parades and all, but it ain't the same. Things change." Suddenly, as if it took all his strength to do so, he tore his eyes away from the leaping flames and glanced out the window into the pouring rain. "Looks like it's going to keep it up all day long," he observed.

That's the way it was with Jack. Just when you thought you had him, when it looked like he was going to open up and let you see right into his soul, you came up against a blank wall. I knew I wasn't going to get anything more out of him that day, so I shoved closer to the stove and thought about what he'd told me. It wasn't much.

I guess I must have fallen asleep, because the next thing I knew it was dark in the room, and when I went to brush my hair out of my eyes I noticed it was dry. There was still some light: I could just make out the outline of the stove with its crack a glowing red crescent in the base and the window opposite me, the one with the single remaining pane of glass, was a grayish square in the black of the wall. I looked up at the chair in which I had last seen Jack sitting. It was empty. I sat up.

"Jack—" I whispered.

"Shhhh!" He was crouching across the room from me, holding his rifle across one knee and watching something through a corner of the broken window. The flames showing through the crack in the stove made his shadow dance along the walls and ceiling.

I had no idea how long he had been squatting there. Minutes crawled by like snakes awakened from their winter sleep, and still he remained motionless, long after my younger muscles would have given away beneath the strain. The rain had slowed to a steady drizzle. Every now and then a bolt of lightning would strike and throw the scene outside the window into blinding brilliance, then darkness would come rushing back in to fill it up and the sky would split apart with a splattering crack of thunder. I could see nothing out there during these times that would explain Jack's alert condition, but I knew there was something, or he wouldn't be there with his white hair falling all about his face and his finger resting on the front trigger of the big Sharps. I breathed as quietly as I could and listened.

Then Jack's buffalo robe was pushed aside and lightning was striking and a figure at least ten feet tall was standing on the threshold with a knife in its hand. Thunder crashed. I thought it was Jack's Sharps and I scrambled to my feet, grabbing for the Winchester I had left to dry leaning against the wall on the other side of the stove. But there was no shooting. When I wheeled to bring my rifle into play, this is what I saw: Jack still in his crouched position beneath the window, his Sharps pointing toward the door; a slim man of medium height standing in the doorway with his hands raised over his head; and, lying on the floor where Jack had shouted for him to drop it, a hunting knife with a long blade. The intruder had shrunk a good four feet since coming into the shack, but that was about all I could tell of him in the poor light. I wouldn't have seen the knife if it weren't for the flames from the stove glinting on its polished surface. Thus seeing that my partner had the situation well in hand, I relaxed my stance, but I kept the Winchester trained on the stranger.

"Boy," Jack addressed me, his voice dead calm, "there's a candle stub in my saddlebags. Light it and put it on the table."

I found it, a two-inch-long lump of wax about as big around as my thumb, and lit it with one of the matches from the saddlebag. A warm yellow glow bloomed over the table and on the faces of the two motionless men. I confess that I gasped when I saw the stranger's features, but I think I covered it up well enough by turning it into a cough.

The stranger was an Indian. He wore a faded calico shirt, denim pants held up by suspenders, and a pair of boots that were a size too big for him; white man's clothes right enough, but his face and hair were straight out of Custer's Last Stand. It was a round face, kind of flat and bony, and framed by hair that was long and loose and black and hanging wet about his shoulders. You've seen it a thousand times, staring out of pictures of adobe villages in parched deserts under a blazing sun, and never thought twice about it. Well, if you were there with us, standing with your gun in your hand in a shack in the rain and that face was in there with you, you'd think about it a second time. And a third. And a fourth. You'd probably go on thinking about it, as I did, until someone's voice broke the crusty silence.

That someone was Jack. Slowly, keeping the huge bore of his buffalo gun trained on the Indian, he rose from his crouch. Standing, he towered over the newcomer by almost half a head. "You savvy American?" he asked.

"I speak English, like you," answered the other. He said it with a kind of smile that made me mad to see it.

"I thought so. Get his knife, boy."

I came forward and scooped up the knife. It was a handsome weapon with a steel blade and a bone handle that seemed to mold itself to your fingers. It hadn't been made on any reservation. I offered it to Jack, but he kept his eyes on our guest. I withdrew it.

Jack said, "Suppose you tell us who you are and what you was planning to do with that there knife."

The irksome smile was still on his lips. "I'm cold, and I'm hungry, and I need a place to rest," he said. "When I saw the horses in the stable, I wasn't sure what to expect. I came prepared."

"Sounds plausible. Too bad I don't believe it."

"What do you believe?"

"I believe the part about you being cold and tired and hungry," said Jack. "But I also believe that you seen your chance to make off with some horses and grub and supplies, and that you come in with that knife just in case one of us didn't see it your way. I believe you would cut your own mother if it meant your staying ahead of whoever's after you. That's what I believe."

The Indian kept quiet during all this, but as Jack went on, the smile faded and his eyes took on a narrow, furtive look, as if searching for an avenue of escape. I realized then that what Jack said was true. When the time came to answer him, however, the hunted look had fled and the smile was back. "And what makes you think I have someone after me?" he asked.

"Someone learned you to talk American," observed the other. "That means you ain't no renegade, and nice, law-abiding injuns don't wander around in the rain on foot and come into strange buildings with weapons in their hands. You're being chased, all right. Question is, by who?"

"How do you know I've been traveling on foot?"

Jack sighed, as if the answer were obvious. "You don't splash mud up to your knees on the back of a nice high horse."

The Indian's eyes flickered downward toward his denims, which—do I have to say it?—were plastered with mud from the knees down, and the smile deepened. "You've a sharp eye, my friend," he said.

"You still ain't told me who you are."

"I'd feel a lot more like talking if I had something in my stomach."

I couldn't believe it. I said, "Will you listen to that gall!"

But Jack only smiled and lowered his rifle. "I reckon we can oblige you there, stranger," he said. "Boy, get yourself dressed and fetch me some water for supper."

I'd forgotten that I wasn't dressed. I drew the blanket I was wearing tighter about my throat. "Aren't you going to check him for any weapons?" I asked.

"Why? You got his knife."

"But he might have a gun!"

Jack gave me an exasperated look. "Now, why would he come traipsing in here with a knife in his hand if he had a gun?"

I hadn't thought of that. I went to get my clothes.

Dressing was awkward, because I was unwilling to take my eyes off the Indian and I kept making sure that Pa's Winchester was still lying on the chair where I'd left it, within easy reach of my right hand should our guest try anything. I use the word "guest" with only a little irony, because that's the way Jack was treating him. He even let him warm himself by the stove while he prepared the skillet for supper. The only visible sign that this was not some social occasion was Jack's Big Fifty leaning against the wall where he could snatch it up on an instant's notice.

"You'd be a sight more comfortable if'n you took off them clothes and let them dry by the stove, like the boy there," suggested Jack.

"Thanks," said the other, but he kept his clothes on.

Supper was a delicious concoction of beans mixed with big square chunks of bacon. I ate with the Winchester lying across my lap, Jack with his Sharps leaning against the table on the far side from the Indian. Afterwards we all sat around the table drinking coffee which Jack had brewed in an old chipped enamel pot he said he had been carrying since the Battle of Pittsburg Landing. Shiloh, he called it. We didn't have any cup for the Indian, so he drank out of a preserve jar from which I had poured the rain water and washed as best I could with a grimy old rag. It didn't slow him down any; he drained it while Jack and I were still blowing on ours to cool it off.

"My name is Logan," he began, fulfilling his part of the bargain he had struck with Jack. "I'm from the Lapwai Reservation in Idaho. I stole a horse there last month and took off for California, but it went lame about five miles back, so I cut its throat and took off on foot. I didn't know there were so few farms in this part of the country, or I'd be sitting a new mount and well on my way to Sacramento by now." He poured himself another jarful of coffee and sat sipping it, his eyes on Jack.

"Why'd you leave the reservation?" asked Jack.

"For the same reason you'd leave a jail cell if someone left the door open." The Indian set his jar on the table and held it between his hands as if to warm them. His eyes were hard. "You don't know what it's like being confined to a few hundred acres of ground just because your skin is darker than your jailers'. One morning I just couldn't take it any more. When I saw that horse tethered in front of the chief's hut, I just mounted it and rode off. I don't think anyone even knew what I was doing until long after I was gone."

"You stole the *chief's* horse?" I asked incredulously.

He turned a poker face on me. "Why not? He's just a sick old man. He won't be needing it any more."

"Why California?" cut in Jack. "Seems to me Canada's a lot closer, and no law can touch you once you cross that border."

"That's what you think. The law in Idaho would just as soon shoot me in Canada as on the reservation. A line on a map means nothing to them."

"Who's after you?" asked Jack.

"Nobody in particular," shrugged the Indian. "I saw a flyer they had out on me in La Grande. Since then I've been able to stay one jump ahead of it. I'm in no real danger as long as I keep moving." He frowned. "That is, I wasn't until now."

"You Shoshone?" said Jack, eyeing the other through narrowed lids.

"Nez Percé."

Jack slapped the table with the flat of his hand. I jumped at the noise. "I might of knowed," he said, laughing. "I seen a lot of your red brothers when I was with the U. S. Army fighting Chief Joseph in '77."

"You were in that?" The Indian looked at him quickly. I didn't like the tone of his voice.

"Chief of scouts, with the rank of lieutenant colonel," nodded Jack. "Was you in it, too?"

The Indian shook his head. "Too young. But my father was. He died three years later in the territorial prison."

"Meanest bunch I ever fought," said the other in a tone of admiration. "Fought like wildcats, they did, and by the time it was over, you couldn't walk your horse across the field without stumbling over a dead injun."

"What do you plan to do with me?" asked Logan, if that was really his name. The switch in subjects was an abrupt one, and it took Jack a second to catch his drift.

"I reckon we'll tie you up for tonight, seeing as how we can't trust you out there with them horses," he said at last. "Boy, fetch me the rope from my saddle."

I brought him the rope. Bending over the Indian, Jack said, "Since you ain't done us no harm, we're going to turn you loose tomorrow. This is just to make sure we keep our scalps tonight."

Five minutes later our visitor was tied into the chair about as tight as he was likely to get, so Jack gathered up his rifle and unrolled his bedding on the floor next to the stove. Since I was the better rested, I volunteered for the first watch. Jack didn't argue. He crawled under his blanket, laid his rifle across his lap, and in less than two minutes he was asleep. That left me sitting across from Logan with my Winchester close at hand and the captured knife lying on the table in front of me. By this time he was asleep too, and snoring quietly. Jack slept until about two o'clock, at which time he got up without having to be awakened and took my place while I got some extra sleep.

The rain had stopped by the next morning. Jack untied Logan's hands long enough for him to eat breakfast with us, then replaced the bonds and directed me to bring our mounts around to the front of the shack. Outside, everything seemed fresh and newly washed. Quartz Mountain rose big and white and dazzling against a pure blue sky, and the birds were singing and using their beaks to clear the drops of water from between their feathers. When I returned to the shack, I found Jack standing in the middle of the floor with his saddlebags over his shoulder, his rifle in one hand and Logan's long-bladed hunting knife in the other.

"Them knots ain't so tight you won't be able to work your way out of them with a little sweat," he told the Indian. "But just in case you get impatient, I'll leave this here." So saying, he bent down and jammed the knife almost up to its hilt in the hard earthen floor at his feet. Then he picked up his saddle and headed out the door. Logan said nothing. He hadn't spoken a word since last night.

"Where to now?" I asked Jack as he was saddling his mule. The burro was already loaded up and ready to go.

"I reckon we'll get back on the old trail and follow it till we spot some fresh signs," he said, and gave the cinch a mighty yank. The mule grunted. "We'll have to scramble to make up for lost time, though. That means no stopping till dark."

"Suits me," I said. "I'm tired of sitting still anyway."

"You're a born hider, boy."

That made me feel proud. I swung into my saddle with a flourish, but my conscience got the better of me and I cast an uneasy glance back toward the shack. "Do you think he'll be all right in there?"

"He'll be fine. Them Nez Percés thrive on hard times." Jack placed his boot in the mule's left stirrup and started to mount.

Then a shot rang out of nowhere and smashed the last pane in the shack's front window into a hundred pieces.

CHAPTER 5

I was too busy trying to control my horse to react to the report and the almost simultaneous crash of the window, but Jack was off his mule and moving before the glass hit the ground.

"Get inside!" He yanked his Sharps from his saddle scabbard, and, in the same movement, slapped his mule sharply on the rump. It brayed indignantly and took off at a lope, half-dragging the little burro behind it at the end of the stout halter. My bay didn't need any such encouragement; as soon as I was off its back, it broke into a gallop and within thirty seconds was running neck-and-neck with the big mule. By this time I was halfway to the door of the shack. Behind me, I heard Jack's Sharps whamming away as he backed toward the building. Two more shots rang out from the surrounding hills, but by that time we were both inside and sitting on the floor on either side of the empty doorway.

"Who in hell is that?" wheezed Jack. He was out of breath from the sudden activity. Well, so was I. He reloaded his rifle with a cartridge he had taken from his jacket pocket.

"I forgot to tell you about him," said the Indian, who had thrown himself to the floor, chair and all, and was struggling to free himself from his bonds. "He's after me."

"I thought you said nobody in particular was chasing you."

"I lied."

"Who is he?" Jack repeated. He kept his right cheek pinned to the wall, watching what he could see of the hilly countryside. If he saw anything, it was from an angle that was closed to me. All I could see were trees and bushes.

"His name is George Crook. He's an Indian policeman from the reservation." Logan grunted and strained, but the ropes didn't appear to be loosening. "How about throwing me that knife?" he said. "I'm a sitting duck here."

"Then waddle out of the way."

The Indian cursed and renewed his struggles.

I said, "Why didn't we make a break for it when we had the chance? We don't owe him anything."

"No good," said Jack. "Too much open territory. He would of picked us off afore we got within a hundred yards of the woods."

"Now we're pinned down good," I grumbled. "We don't even have our mounts."

"They'll be back."

There was another shot, and a bullet splintered the door jamb within an inch of Jack's face. He jerked back.

"He seems awful determined to take you back dead," he said to the Indian. "That must of been a mighty important horse."

"I sort of lied about that, too." Logan had made some headway with the ropes and was working his hands free behind his back. "He's got a special reason to want me dead," he said. "I married his woman."

"I can see how that might rile a man, especially a injun," said Jack. "Anybody with him?"

"Just one. Another policeman by the name of Clyde Pacing Dog."

"Fine."

I wet my lips, which had suddenly gotten very dry. "What's stopping us from turning the Indian over to them? Then they'd have no reason to hold us here."

The Indian ceased struggling.

"Don't count on it," said Jack. "Three dead's a lot neater than just one."

Logan resumed his efforts. In a moment he had his hands free and was working on the knots that bound his legs to the chair. That done, he kicked the chair away and began crawling the long way toward us around the table. His shirt and jeans rustled against the hard earth of the floor. He was almost up to the knife which Jack had thrust into the floor when the hider closed his hand over the hilt. Their eyes met.

Logan said, "You can shoot me if you want, but I'm not going to die unarmed."

There was a moment of silence while Jack took his measure. Then he nodded and let go of the knife. Logan pulled it free, wiped the dirt off on his right sleeve, and returned it to the sheath at his belt.

"Well, what are we going to do now?" I asked.

"Only thing we can do," said Jack. "Wait."

"For what?"

Jack shifted into a sitting position with his back against the wall and laid his Sharps across his lap. "Long as we stay in here, they can't get at us," he explained. "They're going to have to make a move of some kind."

He was right, of course. No other shots came down from the hills, and while it wasn't exactly like sitting in your parlor and reading *Silas Marner,* I admit that I felt pretty secure with the two of us guarding the door and Logan keeping watch through the side window, ready to sing out should either of our visitors try to sneak up on our blind side. We only had one problem, and that was that we couldn't move.

It wasn't a comfortable wait, either. The sun had barely cleared the peak of Quartz Mountain when it began to get hot. By midmorning the grass outside the shack was dry and the birds had stopped singing in order to conserve their energy. The cabin was little enough protection against the stifling heat, but for the two Indians out in the open it must have been unbearable. Beads of sweat formed on my face and bled down into my collar; after a while I gave up wiping them away as a useless effort. Jack, too, was sweating, but the heat didn't seem to tell on him the way it did on me. I suppose he was used to sitting still for hours at a time. The Indian seemed no less content to be sitting there with his knife safely in its sheath and his attention on the scene beyond the window. I guess I was the odd one.

"You in the shack!"

The shout was so unexpected that I nearly jumped to my feet. As it was, I had my legs gathered up under me to do just that when my rifle slid off my lap and I had to catch it before it clattered on the floor. I pressed my head against the wall the way I had seen Jack doing and looked out.

I saw him at the top of the hill, a rider with a rifle braced against his knee so that its barrel stuck straight up into the air above his head. And I saw something else. I saw a white flag fluttering from its muzzle.

Jack had evidently been watching him for some seconds before he had shouted. Anyway, my partner had changed position, and now he was lying on the floor propped up on his elbows and he was drawing a bead on the rider with his Sharps. Logan watched him in silence from his station at the window.

"He's carrying a white flag!" I exclaimed.

"Yeah," said Jack. "Makes a nice target, don't it?" He set the action by pulling the rear trigger and prepared to squeeze the lethal one in front of it.

"You can't do that!" I said. "At least give him a chance to say what he wants to say!"

"Don't listen to him." Logan's voice was hardly more than a whisper. "George Crook's full of tricks."

I don't know if it was me telling him not to or the Indian telling him to go ahead that made Jack change his mind, but after a couple of seconds he raised his cheek from the walnut stock. "What do you want?" he called out to the motionless rider.

The rider shouted down from the hill. "I would like to talk!"

After the echo of his words had died out, Jack replied. "Talk!"

"Not from up here," said the other. "Let me come down."

"Don't let him," warned Logan behind us.

Jack thought for a moment. "All right," he shouted finally. "Come ahead!"

Logan cursed. "You fool! It's just a trick to get us out into the open so the other one can pick us off."

"You can crawl under the table if you want," commented Jack dryly. That quieted him.

We remained where we were as the rider picked his way down toward the shack. He was a tall Indian on a dun-colored horse with a white blaze, and he was wearing buckskin pants and a blue shirt. The shirt, which by federal order had ceased to be the official uniform of the U. S. Cavalry, was worn and faded and patched in several places. He wore a bright red headband, but that was only for decoration because his hair was cut short. His face was dark brown and covered with tiny pits. I figured he must have had smallpox pretty badly at one time. Unlike the somber Indians you read about in dime novels, this one grinned a lot.

"It's Clyde Pacing Dog," said Logan.

Jack waited until he was at the bottom of the hill before he called out to him to stop. Then he rose and stepped cautiously out the door, his Sharps at the ready. Logan and I followed him out. The fugitive's knife was drawn.

Clyde Pacing Dog looked down at us from atop his horse. He kept his free hand on the butt of the revolver he wore low on his right hip. It was a long gun with an ornate grip. "Howdy, Logan," he said to our Indian companion. His voice was cheerful.

The response was grave. "Hello, Clyde. Where's George?"

"He's up there, waiting." The mounted redskin turned in his saddle and pointed back up the hill. I looked up and saw another rider at the top, this one with long hair and a high-crowned hat. That's all I could see of him against the cloudless blue of the sky.

"What you want to talk about?" demanded Jack. He had his rifle trained on Clyde's chest.

"I think that's obvious," said Clyde, grinning. "Turn Logan over to us and you and the boy can go."

"What happens to the injun once you got him?"

The grin widened. "I think that, too, is obvious."

"I don't know," drawled Jack, as if he were having trouble making up his mind. "Somehow it don't seem Christian. I'm a churchgoing man, and it just wouldn't set right if I was to let someone get killed who was in my charge."

"Would you rather be killed along with him?"

"That sounds mighty like a threat."

The grin faded. Now there was only coldness in the Indian's pockmarked features. "Take it or leave it, mister," he said.

Jack started to turn toward Logan. It looked like he was considering the offer. Then, suddenly, and before the Indian could draw his gun, the hider pulled the trigger of his Sharps and it exploded right into Clyde's midsection, catapulting him from his horse and spraying blood and bone and bits of red meat all over. The horse screamed, but Logan grabbed its reins and held it. The sound of the report echoed in the distance long seconds after the Indian was dead.

An animal scream sounded from the top of the hill. I looked up to see George Crook rear his horse and disappear over the bulge.

"I got an idea he'll be back," said Jack.

"I'll let you know when my ears stop ringing," said Logan.

I looked down at the dead Indian, and had to turn to keep from being sick. He wouldn't be grinning any more.

Logan, who had succeeded in bringing the badly frightened horse under control, came over to observe the body. He whistled. "Wouldn't a nice, safe little cannon have done just as well?" he asked.

"What did you do that for?" I raged at Jack. My breakfast was still doing flip-flops in my stomach, but the big danger was past. "He didn't even have a chance to draw."

"That was the idea." Jack placed a fresh cartridge in his rifle and swung the trigger guard back to its original position, slamming shut the breech. Without pausing, he raised the weapon and pointed it at Logan. "Stop right there, injun," he said. There was no anger in his voice; only warning.

The Indian had bent over Clyde Pacing Dog's body and was in the act of reaching for the gun in the dead man's belt. He froze with his hand on the fancy grip and looked at Jack. I braced myself for the roar of the Sharps. You might say I was a little gun shy by this time.

"You'd leave me unarmed?" Logan remained in his bent-forward position, one hand on the gun, the other still holding on to the reins of the captured horse.

"I let you have the knife," said Jack. "That's as far as I go. How do I know you ain't wanted for murder?"

Logan eyed him flatly. "You realize what this means."

"I reckon I do."

"Without weapons, I can't afford to go off on my own after what's happened." The Indian straightened. "From here on in, we're partners."

"I reckon so," said Jack. He lowered the rifle.

"Just a darn second," I put in, turning on Jack. I was still mad and half sick over what had happened to the Indian policeman. "As far as I'm concerned, we'd be a lot better off if Logan got on that horse and rode just as far away from here as it will take him. We don't have time to play hide-and-go-seek with the law. Have you forgotten what we're here for in the first place?"

"You're in it too, son." Logan stroked the horse's white-streaked nose. It had calmed down quite a bit, but it shied from the body of its dead master. "Your friend just did for George Crook's partner. Among the Indian police, that's the same as killing his brother. He won't forget it."

I looked to Jack to see if this were true. He nodded.

"It ain't a case of 'us' and 'him' any more," he said. "Like it or not, we're partners, and that there's what seals the bargain." He nodded toward the grisly thing lying on the ground at our feet. I guess it jogged his memory, because he bent down and unbuckled the gun belt from around the dead man's waist. The leather and cartridges were spattered with blood and bits of flesh, but the gun in the holster had escaped unstained. "Well, will you look at this here," he said, sliding the weapon from its leather sheath.

It was a big revolver, right around thirteen inches long. I mentioned that it had a fancy grip; the brass fittings were bright and shiny and the wooden part was carved all over with intertwining leaves, a pattern that was repeated on the frame of the gun itself. The forward sight had been filed right down to the barrel. I suppose that this was so the gun could be drawn quickly, but it seemed silly because the barrel was so long and unwieldy that it didn't make any difference if part of it caught on the inside of the holster, because you'd be dead before you could lift it into firing position anyway. "Dude's weapons," Pa used to call firearms of this type, reliable enough when you had plenty of time to cock, aim, and fire, but when it came to a real gunfight they were better left in their holsters.

"Colt Transition Model," said Jack, examining it. "Ain't seen one of these in fifteen years. This what they're issuing the Nez Percé law these days?" The question was directed to Logan, who shook his head in reply.

"George Crook receives an annual allotment from the federal government for arms and ammunition, but no one ever sees it," he said. "Most of his men supply their own."

Jack looked from the gun belt in his hands to me and back to the gun belt, then shook his head. He said, "Boy, it'll take a heap of beans and bacon afore you can wear this without it falling down around your knees. You better be satisfied with your Winchester." That suited me fine. I wasn't looking forward to buckling the gory mess around my waist anyway. Slinging the gun belt over his shoulder, Jack reached down again and lifted the Indian's rifle out of the tall grass. It was a Henry with the initials CPD carved crudely into the buttstock. He jacked out all the shells and tossed it to Logan, who caught it in one hand. "Here, injun," said Jack. "If you run into trouble, point it and maybe they'll run away."

"And if they don't?" asked the other, detaching the wilted white banner from the muzzle.

"Then hit them over the head with it and run yourself."

I heard a strangling noise and looked up to see a pair of turkey buzzards flapping and wheeling about the sky in wide circles. I reckon they were about two hundred feet up and coming closer with each pass. How do they always know?

Jack noticed them too. He held up a hand to shield his eyes from the sun's glare and watched their gyrations for a silent moment.

It was a mistake. While the hunter's back was turned, Logan let go of his captured horse and ran at him, swinging the Henry by its barrel so that the butt came around and smashed Jack in the side of the head. That's what I thought happened. In reality, Jack ducked at the last instant so that the club only swept his hat off; at the same time he brought the butt of his own rifle around in a scooping motion and punched it hard into the Indian's stomach. Logan's breath came out in a *woof* and he doubled over and just sort of wilted to the ground. The buzzards, startled by the sudden activity, departed in a flurry of wings. Logan was still lying there gasping for air when Jack placed the muzzle of his Sharps beneath the Indian's nose.

"Injun," he said calmly, "I'd be obliged if you don't do that again. I ain't killed two men in one day since the war, and I ain't sure my conscience can handle it."

I felt pretty foolish standing there with my Winchester in my hands without doing anything to help Jack. In order not to call attention to this idleness on my part, I went over to get the masterless horse before it wandered too far away and brought it back to the front of the shack. I heard more squawking and flapping overhead, but this time I didn't bother to look up. It was obvious that our friends the turkey buzzards had returned, and, what's more, that they'd brought some friends with them. They were just waiting for us to leave so they could swoop down and begin their feast.

By this time, Logan had recovered enough of his faculties to climb to his hands and knees. His body shook some and his face was dead gray, but at least he was breathing easier. Jack watched him in silence.

"You know this injun Crook better than me," he said at last. "What you reckon he'll do now?"

"One of two things." Logan was standing now, unsteady but straight. His color was returning. "He'll either make for the nearest telegraph office and wire for reinforcements, or else decide to take after us alone. I think he's just mean enough to try it without help." He was looking at Jack with unconcealed hostility. I imagine he was devising some new plan to get hold of that Sharps or Clyde's Colt. He wasn't the kind to give up easily.

I said, "Well, there are three of us and only one of him. What's to stop us from laying back somewhere along the trail and bushwhacking him when he comes by?"

Logan favored me with a tolerant smile. It reminded me of a schoolteacher who had just heard a wrong answer from one of his students. "That's been tried before," he said. "All that will gain for us is three graves. Our best bet is to put as many miles between ourselves and here as we can before George decides to come back."

"That's just great," I rejoined. "Except that we've only got one horse."

"Not any more," said Jack. Something in the tone of his voice made me turn and look in the direction in which he was gazing. After a moment I saw Jack's mule come trotting out of the shadow of Quartz Mountain, the little burro scrambling to keep up, its packs jiggling on its back. Behind them, a little more hesitantly, followed my bay. "Told you they'd be back," my partner reminded me.

Jack's mule came up to him readily enough, but I had to chase my horse for a couple of hundred yards before I could get hold of its reins and lead it back to the scene of Clyde Pacing Dog's violent death.

"Come on, injun," said Jack, mounting.

Logan, who had been inspecting the corpse, abandoned it and swung on to the back of his new mount. A moment later we were back on the trail heading north. We had barely reached the top of the hill when the first of the buzzards came flapping down, then another and another. I turned to look back, but by that time all I could see of the dead Indian was a mass of heaving black feathers.

CHAPTER 6

"You're hunting *what?*" The astonishment in Logan's voice unnerved his horse, which gave a little whinny and shied sideways as if it had come close to stepping on a snake. The Indian kept his attention on Jack's chiseled profile.

Jack said nothing. He seldom repeated himself, and never when he was sure the other person had heard him the first time. His eyes never left the trail ahead. Logan turned to me.

"Do you want to explain that, or are you as crazy as he is?"

"It's not so crazy," I said, and related the incident of Bullock's cornfield and barbed-wire fence. When I had finished, Logan smiled that funny smile of his and shook his head slowly.

"My whole life's been one joke after another," he said. "A buffalo hunt isn't going to spoil my record." Those were his last words on the subject, and we proceeded in silence.

We'd been traveling for almost an hour. In order to save time in returning to the old buffalo trail, Jack had plotted a northwesterly course straight across country that I call the "up-and-down" portion of Oregon. I think there are more hills in that area than I've seen anywhere else. Because most of the going was uphill, and because Jack's mule and my horse were already lathered from their riderless run that morning, we got off after the first half hour to lead them and give them a rest, and had only just gotten back into our saddles when Logan asked us our reason for being there. It was during that walk that we had introduced ourselves to him by name.

We had gone another mile when Jack spoke again. "You want to tell me the whole story?" he asked.

"What story?" countered Logan.

"About you and George Crook. And don't tell me again about you hitching up with his woman. I ain't never seen no injun that would cross state lines for the sake of a squaw."

Logan nodded. "I guess you're entitled to an explanation." Then he told us everything. As he spoke, he divided his concentration between the trail ahead and the undulating horizon. Before he was finished he had me doing it as well.

"George Crook owes his position in the Nez Percé Indian police to the simple fact that he's the best tracker in the tribe," he began. "In the three years that he's been the head of the unit, not a single fugitive from the reservation has avoided capture for more than a month. Nor, for that matter, has a single one of those captured been brought back alive. This was all right for the first two years, while the chief was well and able to keep George in his place. But the chief is an old man. When he fell sick last year, George took over the reservation. He explained that he was declaring a kind of martial law to prevent things from falling into disorder, but he wasn't fooling anybody."

He paused, as if expecting comment, but I was too engrossed to interrupt and Jack went on riding in silence as if he weren't listening. I knew better: he'd heard every word.

Logan continued. "For ten months he's held that reservation in the grip of fear. If you have a job, he threatens your home and family unless you turn half your earnings over to him. If your squaw is pretty, he takes her for his own. If you stand up to him, he kills you and claims you were trying to avoid arrest. Escape is impossible. Even if you could get past the armed guard that rides patrol on all the approaches of the reservation, George will track you down sooner or later, and then you're as good as dead.

"The Nez Percé were blessed with an honest Indian agent, Sam Dailey by name. When he got back from Washington last month and heard what was going on at the reservation, he came to talk with George Crook. He demanded to know if the rumors were true. George chose not to answer him, so Dailey stalked out of his hut, muttering something about notifying the army. He was in his buggy and halfway across the reservation when George and five or six of his men caught up to him on horseback and surrounded him. George himself did the killing. Dailey turned to ask him what he wanted and he shot him in the face with a rifle."

Again he stopped. There was a long silence, and I began to wonder if he were going to continue. "Where do you come in?" I prodded.

He said, "I wasn't lying when I said I'd married George Crook's woman. This was two weeks after I bribed one of his guards to let us through the cordon long enough to find a justice of the peace and make it legal. It was second best; the situation on the reservation made the squaw-taking ceremony impossible. George didn't do anything at the time, but after he killed Sam Dailey, he saw his chance for revenge. He reported to the local army post that he'd overheard me threaten the agent for refusing to sell me whiskey shortly before the murder. When they searched my hut, the soldiers found the rifle that had been used in the killing, right where George had planted it.

"I was hunting on the east side of the reservation when I heard they were looking for me. Knowing how a white judge feels when an Indian kills a white man, I didn't stop to explain myself. I grabbed the chief's horse—the fastest animal in the camp—and charged straight through the mounted guard. They fired at me, but I was going too fast for them to draw a bead. I'd still be going if the horse hadn't stepped in a rabbit hole north of Diamond Lake."

"What about your squaw?" asked Jack. It was the first he'd spoken since Logan began his story. "If I was George Crook, I'd put a pistol to her head and promise to squeeze the trigger if you didn't come back nice and peaceful."

"The chief is her uncle," said the Indian. "Even George wouldn't dare threaten her, for fear of uniting the entire tribe

against him. She'll be all right." He spoke with conviction, but
I caught a little note of worry in his voice anyway.

Jack said, "That still don't explain why he'd chase you
across three states."

It took Logan a minute to reply to that. He hadn't forgiven
Jack for that rifle butt in the stomach, and I could tell he
didn't like answering his questions. At last he said, "George
has always been a little afraid of me. I think it's because I
don't push as easily as most of the others. It was all right
when I was on the reservation where he could keep an eye on
me, but now that I'm out of sight he's begun to worry about
his back. I think he'd track me all the way to Mexico if it
meant his peace of mind."

A clump of bushes to the right of the trail rustled suddenly,
and Logan had his knife out and ready to throw before I even
saw any movement. I cast a glance in that direction just in
time to see a rabbit dart out of the bushes and race across the
open field to the north, its feet thudding the ground loudly.
Only then did the Indian return the knife to its sheath. Suddenly I knew why George Crook was afraid of him.

"Did anybody see the murder?" asked Jack. Judging by his
silence of the last few minutes, I had thought he'd lost interest
in the subject, but now I realized that he'd been thinking
about it all this time.

Logan laughed bitterly. "Half the tribe stood by and
watched it happen," he said. "That's how bold George has gotten. He knows there's not a one of them with enough courage
to testify against him. That's why he— What's wrong?"

Jack had dismounted and strode over to where a worm-pit-
ted old telegraph pole was leaning at a precarious angle from
the pile of stones that held it up. It had not been in use for a
long time; its lines were frayed and broken and hanging in
great tangles with the ends buried beneath an inch of dirt.
One side of the pole was worn more than the other, rubbed
smooth and slightly concave. It was this side that Jack was
busy examining.

"What is it, Jack?" I asked.

Jack started back. "Shedding season," he said. "When all that buffalo hair starts coming off it makes them itch. Lot of telegraph lines went down when them big brutes started rubbing their hides against the poles. That one's seen more wear than most." He mounted up and urged his mule forward along the trail.

"Did our buffalo rub that pole?"

He shook his head. "Hard to tell. There's tufts of hair caught in the wood, but it ain't fresh."

"Do you think we've lost him?" I asked. I wasn't sure I wanted to hear the answer.

"Possible," said Jack, and I felt a sinking feeling in the pit of my stomach. "But it ain't likely," he added. That made me feel better.

Thought of the buffalo had driven all memory of the Indian and the story he had told us from my head. When he spoke, it all came rushing back and I was reminded of the danger we were in. "Does this trail pass near any water?" he asked.

"We'll be at the North Umpqua River afore sundown," said Jack in reply.

"Then there's no reason for the buffalo to leave the trail, except to take a short cut to the river."

"He's heading for water," said Jack, "but he'll follow the trail to get there. Nothing short of dynamite will turn a buffalo off of the run he's following. Nothing, except maybe man."

This exchange between two experienced outdoorsmen lifted my spirits considerably. I wasn't about to let things slip back into their pattern of gloomy silence if I could help it. "Jack," I said, "how did you used to hunt buffalo?"

His expression remained unchanged. His eyes were intent on the trail ahead. He said, "That's like asking how you make possum stew. There ain't no one way."

"What was your way?"

"When I was working for the Union Pacific, I'd get five or six good men together, the best I could find from all the outfits, and we'd head out towards buffalo country with enough ammunition to invade Mexico. We took turns cooking so's nobody could complain about the food. One of us drove the wagon.

"A good hunter could drop a hundred, sometimes a hundred and fifty head a day once we found a good-size herd. But there's more to it than just that. You better make that first shot from high ground, else you'll get caught in the stampede. That's what happened to Bart Campbell in '82. Herd just sort of carried him off. We didn't find nothing to bury excepting his hat, so I fixed up a cross and stuck it in the ground and we hung the hat on top. Poor old Bart." He shook his head sadly. "Anyways," he went on, shrugging it off, "once we downed what we was after, we stripped off the hides and loaded them into the wagon. Boy, you ain't worked till you tried skinning a buffalo. You yank and rip and sweat, but that hide won't budge till it's good and ready. And even when you finally get the hide off and lug it back to camp, you still got to stake it out to cure it, and that's almost as hard as skinning if off in the first place. At the end of the first day you'll swear you just plowed six hundred acres of solid rock."

"Good pay?" I asked.

"It don't seem much for the work, but for the time you put in it's high enough. I cleared seven hundred dollars one winter, not counting what I got for the meat I sold to the army and the railroad."

I whistled. "All for just a few months? Seems a man could retire in a couple of years."

"It does seem that way," Jack agreed.

"Why didn't you retire?" I studied his profile, but I could learn nothing from his expression. "Why'd you stick with it so long?"

He rode another fifty feet before answering. "I asked myself that," he said. "More than once. I guess I just never wanted to stop. The money sort of disappeared after a while. I kept on hunting."

Logan made a disdainful snorting sound. I looked at him quickly. "What's the matter with you?"

"Oh, nothing." He was smiling and his eyes were almost closed, like a lizard sunning itself on a flat rock. "I'm just having trouble swallowing these confessions of a great white hunter." His body swung lazily with the motion of his horse.

Jack said nothing. I reckon that after three years of being called a liar and a fool he had acquired a hide almost as thick as that of the animal he was hunting. I hadn't.

"Well, suppose you tell us what it is about my partner's words that bothers you so much?" I snapped.

The Indian retained the mocking expression. I got the feeling there was something else behind it, something I couldn't see. His face was as hard to read as Jack's, but in a different way. "I find it hard," he said, "to see the nobility in a profession that had for its purpose the extermination of an entire species of creature. Ask your friend if he wasn't hired by the federal government to hunt the buffalo to extinction so that the Indians would starve. Get him to tell you about the thousands of tons of meat that lay rotting in the sun while Indian children cried for food. He was killing a lot more than just buffalo. He was killing a whole people." He was raging, but there was no emotion in his voice. There was just nothing.

"There's some truth in that," said Jack. He couldn't have surprised me more if he'd said he was the Emperor of Germany. "Though none of us figured that's what we was doing. And we didn't do it alone, neither. We had help." He leaned to the right to miss a rain gully that snaked its way down the grade up which we were climbing. The mule responded readily and sidestepped it.

"Who?" shot Logan, when Jack didn't continue. "The army?"

"The injuns," said Jack.

Logan reined in with an abruptness that startled his horse, but Jack kept moving. I followed along. I didn't want to miss any of this.

"The buffalo was on its way out long afore the white man come west," Jack continued. "I reckon we just speeded it up. You hear stories about how the injuns used every bit of what they killed, how they used the hides for warmth, the hoofs for glue, the bones for tools and weapons, and ate the meat. Don't believe it. You know how they hunted buffalo?" The question was directed to no one in particular. Logan and I kept silent. The Indian was moving again, but slowly, hanging onto the hider's every word. "As soon as they spotted a good-size herd," Jack went on, "they'd stampede it over a cliff. Two, maybe three thousand head would come pouring down to bust their necks on the rocks at the bottom. The injuns would cut out a dozen or so for their own use and leave the rest to rot. Ask any old brave. They don't lie."

Logan had no reply for that. I didn't think much of him because of his smart mouth, but I will say that he knew the best times to keep it shut.

It was two hours past noon when I heard the sound of running water beyond a wooded hill. This had to be the North Umpqua. After the way Jack had described it, I hadn't exactly been expecting to hear the gentle gurgle of a river winding its lazy way downstream, but I wasn't prepared for this angry roar either. It sounded ominous.

We rode to the top of the hill, where my suspicions were confirmed. Below us, the north branch of the Umpqua River churned its way across the hilly countryside, tumbling down the cataract, tearing away at the twisting banks, exploding toward its destination at the eastern edge of the county. The water smashed against the flat rocks imbedded in the banks and shattered into thousands of tiny droplets, flashing in the sunlight that slanted between the tall evergreens that flanked the river. Branches and grass, torn away in the flood that had accompanied yesterday's rain, were swept along in the powerful current until they disappeared beneath the boiling water at the beginning of the cataract. It was a savage sight.

"This ain't what I expected," said Jack, after we had descended to the water's edge and dismounted to let the animals drink. He had to shout to be heard above the snarling torrent. "Didn't figure the rain to come this far."

"We'll never be able to ford this," said Logan.

"Buffalo must of crossed just afore the rain. He's got the Lord's good will on his side, and that's a fact." Jack took off his hat and bent to bathe his face with a double handful of the fresh clear water. He didn't appear to be frustrated by the setback. I got the impression he would have been disappointed if things had turned out differently. "We'll have to follow her downstream till she settles down." He put his hat back on and mounted, then swung his mule to the right.

Logan appeared agitated. "I don't like it," he said. "It'll slow us down."

Jack stopped and looked down at him. "Think the injun law's still on our tail?"

"You never know with George Crook," said the other, swinging onto the dun's broad back. "He can track an ant across a flat rock, and it won't realize he's there until he steps on it. I'd rather not find out until we're on the other side of the river."

"What does he look like?" I asked. I was the last to step into leather. "I only saw him from a distance."

"He walked into a trap once when he was trailing a killer outside Boise. Four sticks of dynamite went off within six yards of him. The doctors put him back together, but they didn't do a very good job." Logan's voice was grim. "You'll know him by his twisted face."

Jack said, "Well, we're making mighty poor time sitting here jawing," and led the way downstream.

We were in the big pine country now, and much of our journey was in the cooling shade of towering stands of Douglas fir and yellow pine. Wildlife was plentiful; sparrows and chickadees called unmusically to one another and made a lot of noise as they hopped from one branch to the next, and once my bay almost stepped on a porcupine. It snorted and shied as the fat little beast waddled out of the way, its spiny back gleaming. Fish splashed in the river.

Along about five o'clock we began looking for a place to make camp. It was mid-spring, and there was enough daylight for a good two more hours of riding, but Jack said it would be a good idea to stop while we were still in the high country and able to command a good view of the scenery south of the river. We settled on a spot at the top of a hill that was covered with pines and maples on all sides, but from which we could look out and see open country for ten miles in any direction. Jack was especially satisfied with the site, he said, because the thick layer of last year's fallen maple leaves that carpeted the hill made it impossible for anyone to sneak up on us without making noise. "Of course," he added, "you can't never be sure where injuns is concerned."

We ate bacon and fried bread for supper. The latter was a product of the sourdough Jack had made with the flour he had bought at Slauson's Mercantile. Since water was so plentiful, we had coffee to drink as well. I enjoyed it tremendously, because every swallow reminded me of the look on Old Man Slauson's face when Jack thrust the muzzle of his Sharps beneath his flabby chin and asked him for another sack of coffee. Once I even chuckled out loud. Logan looked at me strangely, but I didn't bother to explain myself. It gave me satisfaction to know something he didn't, especially after he'd kept so many secrets from us. Anyway, no one felt much like talking, so when the food was gone and the dishes washed, Jack banked the fire and we climbed into our bedrolls. I was barely settled in when my partners' even breathing told me they were already asleep.

I lay awake for quite a spell, sorting out the events of the past few days in my mind. Just a short while before, I had been biding my time at home, waiting for someone to buy the land so that I could move on to I didn't know where. My plans had been vague. If anybody had told me then that within a week I'd be going on a buffalo hunt, and, what's more, that my companions would include an old drifter and an Indian wanted for murder, I'd have called him a liar. That I'd be hunted as an accessory to a murder was of course inconceivable. Life is strange. In the last three days I had looked down the twin barrels of a farmer's shotgun, seen a man literally blasted into eternity, and been shot at by a

crooked Indian policeman with murder in his heart. For an
eighteen-year-old kid who had thought he had missed the
thrill of the Wild West, that was reason enough to stay awake
nights. But a long day of hard riding and crippling heat had
taken its toll, and I soon joined Jack and Logan in a deep,
blissful sleep.

I awoke hours later with a slight chill in my bones. I
thought groggily about closing the window, then remembered
where I was, and turned over onto my right side. It was a
good thing I did. In the gray starlight, I saw the black outline
of a figure stealing toward me. Something glinted in its left
hand.

I found my voice. "Jack!" I shouted. "Wake up!" Then the
figure was upon me and I was fighting for my life.

He was much stronger than I was. Twice I had hold of his
wrists and twice he pulled them free with little effort, struggling to get a grip on my own limbs. Each time I expected to
feel the burning pain of his knife slicing across my throat. I
suddenly realized that he had no intention of stabbing me; if
he had, I'd have been dead at least three times by now. Then
I remembered the Winchester. Somehow he knew I had it underneath my blanket, and as he held me down with one hand
he was fumbling with the other to get a grip on Pa's rifle.
There was a grunt of triumph, and then I knew he had it. In a
rush I was reminded of Logan's words: *Sooner or later George
will track you down, and then you're as good as dead.*

Thump! It was a dull noise, something like when you give a
green melon a hearty kick with the side of your foot, and then
a loose sack of something sagged across me and lay still. I
looked up to see Jack standing over me, hatless, with his feet
spread apart and his Sharps gripped in both hands like a balancing rod.

"You all right?" he asked.

I nodded uncertainly. "I think so."

Then he slipped his hand beneath the arm of the uncon-
scious man, and it wasn't until he turned him over onto his
back that I realized it was Logan.

My Winchester was lying a couple of feet away where he'd dropped it. I climbed to my feet and picked it up. By this time the Indian was beginning to stir.

The first thing he did upon opening his eyes was turn his head and retch. "Isn't this getting to be sort of a habit?" he gasped after a moment.

"Suppose you tell me what you think you was doing?" demanded Jack. He stood working his rifle in his hands as if he wanted to hit him again.

Logan groaned and put a hand to his head. I reckon Jack had come pretty close to busting his skull with the buttplate of the big Sharps. At last he said, "You've got Clyde Pacing Dog's revolver under your bedroll."

"So?"

"I wasn't planning to leave the boy unarmed. I just wanted to borrow his gun long enough to make you give up the Colt. That seems to be the only way I can get you to listen to reason."

Jack didn't say anything to that. He thrust his rifle under his arm and drew one of the knives from his belt. It was the conventional one, the one I had seen him use before. "See that?" he said. "That's the knife I would of used to stop you." He slipped it back into its sheath and drew the other one. This was the odd-shaped one that had no point. "See that? That's the one I would of used to take your hide off. One's for ripping, the other's for skinning. Cross me again and I'll demonstrate how they work on you."

It was the closest I had ever seen him come to getting angry. His eyes were hard and his voice had an edge that wasn't there normally. I realized then that he was angry for my sake; that while there was nothing you could do to Jack that would disturb his calm, you were taking your life in your hands when you threatened his partner. I'm not ashamed to admit that in that moment I loved him more than I've ever loved any other man in my life.

Logan must have seen it too, because he didn't challenge

him. There was a long silence, and then he said, "Do you still have that candle stub in your saddlebag?"

"I reckon I do," Jack said cautiously. "Why?"

"I'd like to show you something."

Jack nodded to me, and I went over and fetched the item from among his things. I used the still-glowing coals at the bottom of the banked fire to light the wick. Jack stepped back and Logan got up carefully, holding on to his aching head with one hand as if it were going to fall apart. "It's at the bottom of the hill," he said, pointing into the thick growth of pines to the south.

"Lead the way," said Jack. He had his rifle in both hands again and leveled at the Indian.

Logan led us down the slope. It was dark among the pines, and cold; I could feel the dampness of the dew on the fallen leaves as we shushed through them, soaking my pants legs. "Awhile ago I thought I heard something," the Indian was saying, "and I got up to investigate. I didn't see anything. Maybe I was dreaming. We'll know soon enough." At last he stopped in the clearing at the bottom of the hill and knelt down on one knee. We caught up with him a few seconds later.

"There! See it?"

I squatted beside him and tilted the candle flame to within an inch of his pointing finger. In the yellow glow, the hoofprints of an unshod horse showed clearly on the rain-softened patch of bare ground. The nature of the prints, which overlapped and obliterated each other, testified that the rider had stood in the spot for several seconds.

"Those ain't from our mounts," observed Jack.

"You're right there," agreed the Indian. "These belong to George Crook's paint."

CHAPTER 7

We stared in silence at the tracks for a long time. Then a breath of wind stirred and extinguished the candle flame, leaving us in darkness. A chill danced across my shoulders.

"He must of thought we was farther ahead," Jack said quietly. "Rode too close. All the better for us."

"Better?" I echoed. "How?"

"Least we know he's around. We didn't know that before. When do you reckon he'll make his move?" This last was directed at Logan.

The Indian rose, his clothes rustling. "George likes to sneak up on his victims," he answered. "Night's the best time for that."

Jack led the way back up the hill. "We'll set up a lookout from here on in. I'll take the first watch."

The rest of the night was long. Jack took a sitting position against a tree on the south side of the hill, his back to camp and his Sharps across his lap, while Logan and I returned to our bedrolls. It might as well have been me sitting out there for all the sleep I got. George Crook wasn't the only Indian I was worried about; I'd never completely trusted Logan since the first minute I saw him sneaking in through the door of that old line shack with a knife in his hand, and the events of a little while ago had only confirmed my suspicions. After all, we had no proof that the Indian was innocent of murder, or even that he was who he said he was. I lay with my hand curled around the lever of my Winchester just in case he decided to try for it again, but still I didn't sleep.

I was still awake two hours later when Jack came to get me. "Your watch, boy," he said. "Two hours."

I climbed out of my bedroll, bringing my rifle with me.

"You know how to fire that thing, boy?"

"Sure," I said. "You think I've never gone hunting?"

He grunted. "We're the ones being hunted now, boy. Get to it. The injun'll relieve you in two hours."

"Him!" I exclaimed. "You're not going to give him a gun!"

"Just get out there."

I left him reluctantly and sat down where Jack had been. I was wide awake. In front of me, the ground dropped off at a forty-five-degree angle for about two hundred yards, where, in the blackness of the night, it leveled out into fields carpeted with tall grass. It was silent in the woods. Every now and then a breeze would hiss through the tops of the tall pines and set the leaves on the maples to rattling, but these sounds were of short duration and served only to make the long stillnesses in between seem more acute. I peopled the area around me with a thousand nameless terrors. When an owl began hooting a few trees from where I sat, I shot bolt upright, my rifle in hand, and from then on every little sound was enough to start my heart pounding as if it were trying to beat a hole in my chest. Those two hours out in the woods were the most nerve-racking I have ever spent anywhere.

They passed, however, and I was just thinking about heading back to camp when I heard a leaf crunch behind me. My blood froze. I swung my Winchester around, but a hand shot out and closed around the barrel.

"If I were George Crook," whispered a voice, "you'd be dead."

It was Logan, standing beside the tree. He was wearing Clyde Pacing Dog's gun belt, and in his hands he held the Henry that Jack had given him. Something about the way he handled it told me it was loaded. So Jack had decided to arm him, after all. I got to my feet, eyeing him warily.

"Don't worry," he said in that same low whisper. "I'm saving my ammunition for George Crook."

I struck off for camp without replying and left him there.

The morning chill was already burned off when I rolled out from under my blanket. Jack was loading the burro and Logan was tending the fire. He was still wearing the Colt, only now he had the butt turned forward to accommodate his left-handed draw. Dark stains showed on the leather where he had been unable to cleanse it completely of blood.

"Why didn't somebody wake me?" I asked, blinking. I had finally gotten to sleep just before dawn and had not opened my eyes since.

"No need," said Jack. "We wanted plenty of light afore we left. No sense making it easy for our friend to bushwhack us."

I nodded. "See anything last night?" I asked Logan.

"Not a thing." The Indian blew the dust from Jack's skillet and placed it atop the fire. "He's playing a waiting game to make us nervous. He only does that when he's sure he can't lose."

I shook the cobwebs out of my head and gathered up my bedroll, making sure the Winchester was wrapped up tightly. Jack watched me.

"What you keep that Winchester gift-wrapped for, boy?" he asked.

"I don't have a scabbard," I said. "No place else to carry it."

"Ain't too handy. What if we get jumped?"

"I never thought of that," I admitted.

"What makes you think you can drop a man with that thing anyway? You any kind of shot?"

"I've killed my share of rabbits with it. My pa used to say it was the best gun ever made."

"Maybe so," said Jack. He finished securing the bundles on the burro's back and slipped his own rifle from his saddle scabbard. "A Sharps, now; there's a weapon for a man."

"What are you going to do?" I asked.

"About time you learned to fire this gun, boy. You never know when you might need it." He tossed the rifle its last two feet into my hands. I nearly dropped it. It was even heavier than it appeared, fully twice the weight of my shorter carbine, and it had a curious kind of balance I was unfamiliar with. I turned it over respectfully and admired its trim lines.

Jack stepped to the edge of the clearing. He scanned the dense woods for a moment, then pointed down the hill. "See that pine? The one with the busted branch?" I squinted at a twisted yellow pine standing fifty yards away. It was dead at the top and it had a splintered branch about halfway up its trunk. I nodded and hoisted the rifle to my shoulder.

"Just a minute," Jack said. He curled a long arm around my shoulders and pulled the rear trigger. It responded with a sharp click. "Go to it, boy," he said, withdrawing his hand.

I rested my cheek on the battered stock and took aim. It wasn't easy, with the heavy barrel pulling forward and down all the time, but at last I was able to draw a steady bead. I rested my finger on the front trigger.

The rifle exploded, throwing me onto my backside. Leaves and needles floated down all around me.

"What happened?" I gasped. I couldn't breathe and my ears were ringing. I thought my shoulder was broken.

Jack's voice fell faintly on my whining ears. "You missed by a country mile, son. That's what happened."

I sat up feebly, the smoking rifle across my lap. "I didn't even touch the trigger!"

"You touched it," he said. There was a mischievous glint in his eye. "I forgot to tell you; after you pull the hind trigger, it don't take much more than a slight breeze to set off the front one." He chuckled softly and reached out a hand to help me to my feet.

I slapped it aside. "Very funny!" I got up, swaying on unsteady legs. The air stank of gunsmoke. "How come you didn't tell me it was a hair trigger? I could have busted my back!"

"Well, maybe not your back." He took back the rifle and strode over to his mule. "You should of asked me afore you fired it. Don't never trust a strange gun."

"That's one hell of a firearm," said Logan, who was busy watching over the skillet in the campfire. The smell of cooking beans mingled with the acrid odor of smokeless powder.

"Yeah." Jack extracted a bore mop and a can of oil from his saddlebags and began cleaning his rifle barrel. "You can't beat a Big Fifty for range. Old pard of mine bought fifteen of them back in '79 and lit out for New Mexico. Figured he'd sell them for twice what he paid in the Lincoln County War."

"What happened?" I asked sulkily. I hadn't forgiven him for his little joke.

He snorted. "Nothing. War was over by the time he got there." He lapsed into silence, and I thought he'd come to the end of his story. Then: "They caught him five years later in Arizona selling guns to Geronimo. Hung him."

Logan stood and stretched. "If you two are through playing with guns," he said, "breakfast is ready."

I didn't much like the way the Indian made breakfast. The bacon was so crisp it snapped in my fingers, the way I hated it, and the beans were too dry. The coffee tasted like iodine. I ate without complaining; kicking about the food is the quickest way I know of being made the cook the next time around.

"Where to now?" asked Logan after we had broken camp and were seated astride our mounts once again. Armed to the teeth as he was, with Clyde's revolver strapped to his hip and the Henry slung over his left shoulder, he looked much more like a savage Indian.

"Just because he's close don't mean our plans have changed none," said Jack. "Downriver."

Jack had been as right about the river as he was about most other things. As we left the hilly country behind us, the pull on the water lessened and the explosive rush gradually decreased, until, late in the morning, we stopped and faced a wide expanse of gently flowing water. Stretching before us, it looked like a small lake.

"This is it," said Jack. "It won't get no calmer than this."

"It looks deep," I ventured.

"Nope. See that brown color? That's mud. Can't be no more than four foot deep."

Logan looked doubtful. "It's wider than I thought it would be," he said. "I hope this dun is used to crossing water."

"Any horse worth its price will cross."

That must have been good enough for the Indian, because he hit the water first, slapping his animal on the rump so that it didn't have time to think about balking. Jack and I were right behind him. Actually, it was a little deeper than the four feet Jack had calculated—I soon became soaked to the hips—but the current wasn't too strong and the bay, which had already proved itself in the swifter waters of the South Umpqua during heavy rainfall, had no trouble keeping its footing. Beneath me, the thrashing of its muscular legs sounded like explosions.

The explosions became more distinct. I raised my head, listening. I suddenly realized that the sounds were not coming from beneath me, but from behind. They were rifle reports.

I twisted around, squinting in the flying water to see where the shots were coming from, but my horse, sensing trouble, broke into a panicky lunge and kept me from getting a good fix on the tree-lined bank. I leaned forward again and dug my heels into its barrel sides for all it was worth. Bullets smacked the water all around us.

Jack was shouting something; I couldn't make it out. I whipped my bay forward through the exploding water, not knowing where the opposite bank lay, nor even in which direction I was heading. I had lost all sense of time and place.

An eternity later I felt the riverbed sloping upward and the water begin to recede. Hoofs scraped at the bank, found a footing. At last we lurched up and out of the river.

"Kick it, boy!"

I didn't wait to find out where Jack was calling from. I did what he said and we took off, making fantastic time now that we were free of the river's drag. I could still hear the rifle discharging behind me, but I knew we were well out of range.

Up ahead, I spotted a cloud of dust and took off in that direction. It led me around a small clump of trees and over a low hill. In the hollow beyond, Jack, his mule galloping like nothing I'd ever seen, was tearing across the countryside with Logan running a close second. Jack had let loose of the burro; although it was running as fast as its spindly legs would carry it, it was falling behind rapidly. I caught up with it and took hold of its flying halter. It was then that I noticed it had lost its load. But I held onto it and hightailed it in my partners' wake.

We must have gone two miles before Jack and Logan finally slowed to a walk. I pulled alongside of Jack, my horse heaving beneath me.

"You all in one piece, boy?" Jack and his mule were wet, but the dust they had kicked up since leaving the river had stuck to them grittily. His buckskins looked like sandpaper. I suppose I didn't look much better. He was looking at me closely.

"I'm all right," I panted. I was nearly as short of breath as my bay. "What happened?"

"George Crook happened." Logan's tone was bitter. "I should have figured he'd pull something like this."

"That's right," agreed Jack. "There ain't no better time to kill something than when it's thigh-deep in water. That's how injuns hunt deer."

"What do we do now?" I put in.

Jack spat out a few grains of dust. "We're safe for now. The injun's got to cross the river, too. Besides, he don't cotton to the idea of taking on three men—two men and a boy, that is —head on. Otherwise we'd of heard from him afore this."

"Don't bet on it," said Logan. "If he figured there was no other way to do it, George would take on the whole U. S. Army. He's been playing it safe because he thought he had us where he wanted us. Not any more. He's mad now."

"So what's his next move?" I asked him.

"I don't know." The Indian's expression was grave. "That's what worries me; I don't have the slightest idea what he'll do next."

The burro brayed loudly and shook itself, drenching me. I informed Jack of the loss of our supplies.

"Strap broke in midstream," he said. "That's why I turned him loose. We got to stop in Reuben and pick up some more grub." He looked at me out of the corner of his eye. "For somebody who was dead set against me spending a dollar for that critter, you sure was quick to grab hold of him when it looked like we was going to lose him."

I had to smile at that. I said, "He's proved himself. I reckon I was wrong."

"Just goes to show you," said Jack.

I looked at him, but he had already fallen back into his habit of searching the ground all around him for signs. He had meant something more than his words implied; I was sure of that, although I wasn't sure what it was. For some reason I felt that I had just been given a rare compliment.

We had been walking our mounts for several minutes when I realized my bay was limping. I got off to look it over, and found that its right thigh was covered with blood. A bullet had left a crease six inches long and nearly half an inch wide less than a hand above its leg, and it was bleeding freely all down the right side. The flesh flinched when I touched it.

"Hold him there," said Logan, and dismounted. I thought that he was going to come over and examine the wound for himself, but instead he left us and struck out on foot. He wandered in a seemingly aimless fashion for ten minutes, head down, studying the ground and swinging his feet in a circular motion to separate the tall weeds that covered it. The land where we were had been farmed at some time. Hard stumps of dry old cornstalks showed here and there among the choking weeds, but it was obvious that it had been many years since the field had been used for anything constructive. I grew impatient.

"What's he looking for?" I asked Jack.

The old hider was studying the horizon. I don't think there was ever a minute when his mind wasn't on that buffalo. "If he wanted you to know," he said, "I reckon he'd tell you." I got the impression he knew the answer, which annoyed me.

Nothing in this world can make you feel more ignorant than the conviction that everyone knows what's going on but you.

Logan had found something. He bent and rummaged through the grass with both hands for a moment, then straightened and began striding back toward us. He had something in his hand.

"Yarrow," he said when he got to within earshot, triumphantly waving a handful of green stalks of something. "You usually find it in old fields."

"You reckon you got enough?" said Jack, studying the fernlike plants in the Indian's hand. "That bay is bleeding like a stuck pig."

"This will do it." Logan got out Jack's little skillet and set it on the ground. Squatting, he placed the fuzzy leaves in the bottom and used the butt of his revolver to grind them into a pasty substance somewhat resembling overcooked spinach. The plant had a pungent, medicinal odor that reminded me of the inside of Doc Ingersoll's office back home. "Hold on to the horse," Logan told me as he got to his feet.

He used the water from his canteen to cleanse the wound. Then, as I held on to the bridle, the Indian took a handful of the green mess and smeared it right into the open cavity. The bay whinnied in pain and tried to rear, but I dug my heels into the earth and held on. Logan stood back while it kicked out with the injured leg in an attempt to drive him away. When it stopped, he moved in again and finished applying the last of the yarrow. Finally he untied the kerchief from around his neck and tied it loosely around the torn thigh to hold the poultice in place.

"What is that stuff?" I asked when he was finished.

Jack supplied the answer. "In Texas they call it milfoil," he explained. "Up here it's yarrow. Injuns been using it to nurse their wounds for hundreds of years. It stops the bleeding and makes healing quicker."

"Does it really work?"

"Sometimes." This time it was Logan who spoke. "At the end of the Nez Percé War, there was not a single stalk of yarrow to be found in Idaho for a hundred miles. It had all been used to heal wounds put there by the pony soldiers." He was looking at Jack. His expression was the same as it had been when he was talking about the extermination of the buffalo.

Jack seemed unmoved by the thinly disguised accusation. "You'd best lead that horse from here on in, boy," he advised me. "We'll see about getting you a good one once we get to Reuben."

I shook my head. "I started with him, and I'm going to finish with him," I said.

"Out here, you got to have a mount you can depend on. You ain't doing him no favors by asking him to do something he ain't up to." His eyes slid toward his mule. "Mule saved me from a grizzly once. Kept him busy while I clumb a tree."

"Is that how he lost his ear?"

"Yeah. See them claw marks on his flanks? Wished I had some milfoil with me that time. Stayed up with him all night. He pulled through, but just barely." The mule must have known what he was talking about, because it gave its master a haughty, sideways look, as if warning him to watch his tongue. They were a lot alike, the animal and the man.

I said, "Then you should know how I feel about the bay."

"Nope. If we was out in the open when it happened, with a buffalo in front and a injun behind, I would of put a bullet through his head and left him there. When it's a matter of dying with him or living without him, I'll choose living every time."

I stroked the bay's neck. It stepped closer and rooted its nose under my hand. "He's a healthy horse," I said. "He'll heal."

Jack said, "Well, I hope he's healthy enough to heal afore we get to town," and swung up into his saddle. "That's where we're trading him in." He kneed the mule forward.

I wanted to protest, but no words came. I turned to the Indian, who was just mounting. "Logan." I guess some of my frustration showed in my voice, because he shot me a quick, hostile look. I softened my tone. "Thanks."

"Forget it," he said, and he was off in Jack's path.

But I would not forget it. I had noted the gentle, almost reverent way he had ministered to my injured mount, and while I wasn't ready to trust him completely, I thought a lot better of him from that time on. No, I said to myself as I led my horse onward, the Indian was not all bad.

CHAPTER 8

I had been to Reuben once before, when Pa had gone there to see a lawyer about ironing out some problems with Olaf Peterson next door over the ownership of six acres along our western property line. I remembered it as a big town compared to Citadel, with brick buildings three and four stories tall and a street so wide you could sling a dead cat from one side to the other without breaking a window. That's if you could ever find a lull in the traffic long enough to sling it without taking the chance of having it land in someone's buggy as it rattled past. It was that busy most of the time.

The sun was a pink glow in the western sky when we came within sight of the Presbyterian church, which at dusk was hung with colored lanterns that could be seen for miles. By the time we reached the town itself, the street lamps were burning and the faces of the buildings that lined the main street were ghostly white. There were people all over the place. They thronged the sidewalks and milled around in the street, making it difficult for us to maneuver our mounts through the heavy traffic. Twice we were forced to stop while a gang of fifteen or twenty people trickled by. Logan cursed them bitterly, but Jack, who had once been forced to stop a supply wagon for twelve hours while a herd of buffalo rumbled past, took it all in his stride. It was a strange sort of traffic, because it all seemed to be flowing in one direction. Most of the congestion seemed to center around a building at the north end of the street. It was lit with flaming torches, but the crowd was so thick in that area that it was impossible to see what was drawing them there.

"I'll meet you north of town." Logan, who had gotten off earlier to lead his horse beside Jack and me, mounted again and gathered up his reins.

"What's wrong?" asked Jack.

"Too many people. I can't take a chance on someone recognizing me from that wanted circular." He gave his reins a flip and trotted off down the street. Soon he was lost among the wagons and buggies at the other end.

"Think we'll see him again?" I asked Jack.

He shrugged. "Reckon we won't know for sure till we get north of town."

The sign on a two-story brick building on the right side of the street read "Reuben Emporium." Jack and I stopped and looped our reins around the rail in front, then went in.

The storekeeper was a middle-aged woman with a heavy, freckled face and hair the color of rusted steel. From her Jack ordered coffee, a sack of salted beef, another of dried apples, five pounds of potatoes, a wedge of cheese, a canned ham, and, wonder of wonders, four cans of peaches. He asked her if she had any sourdough starter and she said that she didn't, so he didn't bother to order flour. When the items were before him on the counter, he reached for the wad of bills in his hip pocket and said, "Lot of commotion up the street. Medicine show in town?"

The woman looked at him suspiciously. "Where you been, mister?" She had a voice like a bull's bellow.

"South. Why?"

"I guess you didn't hear about it then. Ben Granger and his gang tried to hold up the bank this morning. The law was waiting for 'em when they come out. They got the bodies laid out there on the sidewalk in front of the undertaker's place."

"I'll be damned," said Jack. "Ben too?"

She nodded, and jerked her head toward the front window, through which we could see the torches burning two blocks up the street. "It's been like that all day. Folks coming from miles around to see 'em."

Jack paid for the food and we carried it out. We had barely finished loading the burro when he left it and began striding up the street. "Wait here," he said.

"Where are you going?" I called.

"To pay my respects to Ben Granger. What else?"

I hesitated only a second, then took off on his heels.

They had the bodies, stripped clean and only half covered by sheets, propped up on wooden slabs on the boardwalk. The crowd pressed forward to get a better look at the bullet-riddled corpses of Ben Granger and his brothers Bob and Charlie, ignoring the attempts of stern-faced men with badges and shotguns to keep them back. I recognized the Granger brothers from pictures I had seen of them on wanted posters and in the papers, but I needed Jack's help to identify the bodies of gang menbers Al Walker and Pima Pete Lindquist. The crowd laughed when a photographer who had set up his boxlike camera in front of the display told the dead men to hold still, and gasped when the powder in the flashpan went up in a blue-white blaze of light. Nearby, a small man with a round face whom I took to be the undertaker stood in the doorway of his shop and beamed at all the free publicity.

"Get away from there, you son of a bitch." A big lawman with a white handlebar moustache and a huge belly that hung over his belt used the barrel of his sawed-off shotgun to push away a souvenir hunter who had tried to cut off a curl of Ben Granger's beard with a penknife. The offender, a dapper drummer-type, looked as if he were going to put up a fight, but then his eyes fell to the shotgun and he just sort of melted back into the crowd.

"Where's Billy?" Jack asked the man with the shotgun.

The lawman started and swung his weapon around, then relaxed when he saw no threat in the gaunt old man. "He's in the jail," he said gruffly. "We didn't kill him. But that's just a minor technicality."

"Looks like you got your hands full," said Jack.

"Mister," said the fat man, pushing his Stetson back on his head with the shotgun barrel, "you don't know the half of it.

This morning I caught a guy tryin' to saw off one of Pima Pete's fingers with a Bowie knife. I kicked him in the ass and took the knife away from him. That's the way it's been all day long."

"How much longer they going to be here?"

"Not long, I hope. They're startin' to smell. Ma Granger and her brothers is comin' in tonight to take 'em back to Crawfordsville for buryin'. I expect Ben and Bob and Charlie'll be in frock coats and starched collars by that time. I don't know about the others. Pauper's burial, I reckon." He spat a brown jet of tobacco that narrowly missed the glossy boot of a dandy standing on the edge of the crowd.

"How about the old man?" asked Jack.

"Eustace? Hell, he's been dead five years. Had a stroke right after Billy left home to join his brothers. Spent them last two years in bed. Ma's been runnin' the farm ever since. —Lady, if you ain't seen it by now, you're not about to ever." This last comment was directed at a fat, well-dressed woman who had been about to pull the sheet from the bandit chief's naked body.

She said, "Well!" gave the lawman an uppity look, turned, and flounced away, the feathers in her hat bouncing.

Jack shook his head glumly. "Things ain't like they was," he said.

"Ain't it the truth?" returned the other. "Yesterday, these bastards would of wet their pants if Ben or any of his brothers was just to say hello. Now look at 'em, flockin' around like a bunch of buzzards. Well, I only got a month to go afore I retire, and then they can all go to hell."

"What happened this morning?" Jack asked him.

The fat man wobbled his chew around in his mouth as if the taste had suddenly gone bad. "I wasn't on duty," he said. "They tell me Birdie Flatt from the bakery reported the bank door locked and the shades drawn five minutes after it was supposed to open. All the law in town was out front when the gang hit the street. Dick, there, tells me it was Billy fired first. Rudy says it was Ben. Anyhow, a stray bullet hit Old Man

Willis smack between the eyes when he come out of his shop to unroll his awning. Then everybody opened up. Afterwards they found Billy hidin' behind a rain barrel in the alley next to the bank. He's locked up on a charge of murder for Old Man Willis, and the talk is they're gonna hurry up his trial afore his ma can hire a lawyer to get him a change of venue."

"Must of been quite a shooting match," said Jack. "Wished I was here to see it."

"You ought to be glad you wasn't, mister. If you was, chances are you'd be lyin' here alongside of these others, there was that much lead throwed." He put his big hand on the shoulder of a little boy who had wandered too close to the body and steered him in the other direction, propelling him forward with a playful slap on the rump.

"Who's your boss these days?" asked Jack.

"Fellow name of Bud Fowler." The man with the shotgun chewed slowly. "He was sheriff six years, then two years ago they went and made him constable, as if that makes any difference. Good man, but he takes his job too serious to my way of thinkin'."

"Bud Fowler," echoed the other, thoughtfully. "Ain't he the one led the posse that got Red Brannigan down in Mexico?"

"That's him. He was a U.S. marshal then, workin' out of Las Cruces. Got a warrant and tracked him down to a saloon owned by a half-breed in Juárez. Brannigan got two of 'em, but Fowler got Brannigan. Got the half-breed, too, when he come up from behind the piano with a scattergun. Made the papers back east with that stunt." He was chewing his plug a mile a minute now. "Yeah, Bud was one hell of a man in them days. Still is."

"What was the posse doing all this time?" I asked.

He jumped a little, and stared at me as if he hadn't noticed me standing there before. But his eyes slid away without answering my question. I got the feeling that I had stepped on the part of the legend that everyone had agreed to leave alone. I kept my mouth shut after that.

"That must of been fifteen years ago," said Jack.

"More like twenty," said the lawman. "Bud's getting on, and he's got the rheumatism in his fingers, but don't sell him short. He's hell with that scattergun of his. The rest of us carry 'em for looks." He eyed his companion with new interest. "I don't believe I caught your name, stranger."

"You didn't," said Jack. Their eyes met, and the other accepted the answer without comment. They were from the same generation. They understood each other.

"Eustace Granger was with me at Antietam," Jack told me after we had left the old lawman to cope with the unruly crowd. "Grapeshot snatched off his right hand when he was lifting it to signal charge. Seen him again ten years later hide-hunting in Kansas. He had a hook by then. He could skin three buffalo while the rest of us was still cutting on the first one. Had his family with him; I reckon Ben was about fifteen years old at that time, Bob and Charlie about twelve and ten. Last time I seen Billy, his ma was bouncing him on her lap. Ben and Bob never was no good. Eustace used to beat them with a razor strap when he caught them stealing, but I reckon that just made them harder to handle. Charlie I don't know about. Maybe he just went along with his brothers. By the time Billy growed up, robbing banks must of seemed like the family profession. Shame. Eustace was about the most law-abiding man I ever knowed. You can't never tell how far the acorn will drop from the tree."

Our next stop was the livery stable. Despite my protests, Jack made me bring the injured bay to the front of the long low building that stood on a side street just off the main gut while he went in to fetch the owner. He came out a moment later with a narrow-faced old man at his side who wore a battered derby and a dirty vest over an undershirt that looked like it had not been white in many months. When he got close, I noticed that he stank of stale sweat and whiskey. I admit that after four days on horseback Jack and I didn't smell much better, but at least we had an excuse. He walked around the horse slowly, paused when he came to the bandage around its right thigh, then moved on. He got down and felt each of its legs from hock to hoof, then stood and pulled the bay's lips away from its teeth to check them too. When he was finished he wiped his hands off on his undershirt, hooked his thumbs in the armholes of his vest, and scowled as if deep in thought.

"Give you twenty dollars for him," he said at last.

"Twenty dollars!" I howled. "I wouldn't sell his bridle for that!"

"Would of give you twenty-five if not for that there gash on his right thigh. Spoils his looks."

"Ain't looking for money," Jack said calmly. "Looking for a trade. What you got that's decent?"

The stable owner jerked his head toward the darkness inside the building. "Got a mustang I took for what was owed me. Belonged to a tinhorn gambler that got hisself shot over to the saloon. Fine animal. Let you have him for the bay and eighty dollars."

"Bring him out," said Jack.

The owner stepped into the building. He reappeared a couple of minutes later leading a handsome animal with a mahogany brown coat and a star-shaped blaze between its eyes. It wasn't much bigger than a pony. I could tell by its prancing steps that it was a troublemaker.

Jack stood back while I looked it over. It stamped its hoofs nervously when I examined its legs and it wouldn't let me get a look at its teeth, but that was all right because it was obvious that the animal was less than three years old. I said, "That bay is worth fifty dollars anywhere. I'll trade you even up for the mustang."

The stable owner shook his head and scowled like a cigar-store Indian. "I got more into him than that in feed. And your plug ain't worth no more than thirty even without the cut. Gimme the bay and seventy dollars and the mustang's yours."

"Hogwash," I said. "You haven't had him more than a week or he'd be sold already. The bay, and ten dollars. That's ten dollars pure profit."

"Fifty dollars," said the owner. "If you throw in the saddle."

I shook my head. "Twenty dollars. No saddle."

He scowled harder and dug his thumbs deeper into the armholes of his vest. Finally he said, "All right, no saddle. But make it thirty."

"Twenty-five."

"Thirty. My last offer."

I glanced over at Jack, but his face was a mask. I nodded. "Thirty it is," I said, and paid him. I removed the saddle from the bay's back and slipped the bridle off over its head. As I did so, I let my hand brush its nose. It tried to nuzzle closer, but by that time the stable owner had a grip on its mane and was leading it toward the open door of the stable. I put a hand on his arm, stopping him. "Here's five dollars." I handed him a bill. "That's for the vet. I'll be coming through again on my way home, and if I find out you didn't get that cut looked at, I'll take you to court for inhuman cruelty to an animal."

"So what?" he said. "It ain't no crime."

"Maybe not," I agreed. "But how long do you think you can continue to do business once the citizens of this town find out how you treat the animals in your care?"

His expression didn't change, but this time I thought I caught a glint of fear in his rheumy eyes. "I'll get you the bill of sale," he mumbled, and led Pa's bay into the gloom beyond the street lamp.

"Pretty slick piece of horse trading," Jack commented as I was putting the bridle on the mustang. It shook its head and nickered, but I finally managed to secure the harness and force the bit into its mouth.

"I learned from the best," I said, bending down to pick up my saddle. "My pa never was worth shucks as a farmer, but he could outtrade old P. T. Barnum himself when he was sober."

I gathered the saddle in my arms and was about to stand up with it when suddenly I felt a pain in my backside as if somebody had pinched it with a pair of pliers. I cried out and fell sprawling across the saddle. The next thing I heard was Jack laughing. It was the first time I'd heard him do that. I lifted myself onto one elbow and looked behind me. That's when I saw that he wasn't alone in his mirth. Beside him, the mustang was tossing its head, snorting and neighing at its little triumph. I had been bitten.

I had my new mount saddled and had ridden it to the emporium to get the feel of it when Jack arrived on foot and dropped a bombshell.

"Let's pay a visit to the law," he said.

"How come?" I asked, dismounting. For an instant I wondered if he were thinking of turning Logan in, and discarded the thought in the same instant.

"I been going about this all wrong," he replied. "If this Fowler is as sharp as he's made out to be, he can tell us all we want to know about our buffalo."

I said, "Are you crazy? They'll lock us up!" But by that time he was halfway across the street and within spitting distance of the stone building marked "Constable's Office," and I had to run to catch up.

Despite the newfangled title painted on the big front window, the constable's office was a stone building of a type that had not been built in the area for at least fifty years, and it looked just stubborn enough to stand for the next hundred, unless somebody were to toss ten pounds of dynamite in through the front door. Inside, the walls were pine paneled and the floor was constructed of wide wooden planks scarred all over with burn marks from the hundreds of cigars and cigarettes that had been crushed out on them over a number of years. On the back wall, where no visitor could fail to see it upon entering, hung a yellowed old newspaper in a glass frame. I had to step closer to be able to read it in the dim light of the one kerosene lamp that burned atop the paper-cluttered desk in the corner. It was a copy of the Las Cruces *Bulletin* dated June 23, 1880, and the headline across the top of the page read: "Fowler Kills Two in Juarez Shoot-Out." Well, I thought, maybe there was some truth to the legend after all.

To the left, beyond the reach of the lamplight, I saw the

yawning black caves of the jail cells. One of them was occupied; although I couldn't see inside, I heard the unmistakable creak of a body turning over on an iron cot when we came in. The other occupant of the building, a young man in his shirtsleeves with a star-shaped badge pinned to his breast pocket, sat behind the desk. He had his nose buried in a dime novel with a gaudy orange cover. He looked up as we approached the desk and laid the book face-down on the desk. I saw him stiffen when his eyes fell to the Sharps Jack was carrying.

"You the constable?" asked Jack.

He shook his head quickly. "He's across the street, eating supper." There was a catch in his voice. I reckoned he thought it was somebody come to bust Billy out of jail.

"Know when he'll be back? I'd like to ask him a question."

"He—he should be back any time, mister. Maybe I can help?" I could tell that was the last thing he wanted to do. He was the excitable type, kind of pale and sickly and with eyes that darted this way and that constantly as if looking for an escape route. There were shallow depressions on each side of his nose that looked as if they had been made by the nose-piece of a pair of wire-rimmed spectacles, though there was no other sign of them on his person. I didn't much like the whole setup.

Jack rested the butt of his rifle on the floor. If this were meant to put the other at his ease, it didn't work. He remained as jumpy as he had been. Jack was about to speak when we heard a heavy foot on the threshold and turned around. It was the constable.

There was something about the man that pointed him out as an officer of the law. Stout but solid-looking, he wore a dark gray three-piece suit with matching Stetson and carried a sawed-off shotgun. His face was broad and florid and showed every line of his fifty-plus years, along with a couple of others that had at one time been prominent scars. A gray handlebar moustache dipped down to cover his mouth. That didn't matter, though, because the stormy nature of his deep-set eyes was expression enough. Two points of a tin star showed from beneath his coat.

"Rick—" he said gruffly, then noticed us. "You gents got business?"

"It can wait," said Jack. "Go ahead with your own."

The constable squinted suspiciously at my partner for a long moment. "Ain't seen you around here, mister. The kid neither."

"Just got in."

The suspicion in the lawman's dark eyes sharpened. When he spoke this time, it was in a low, wary voice. "You belong to that mule and burro tied up in front of the emporium?"

I looked at Jack. Now there was suspicion in his face too. I could almost see the wheels turning. "They're mine," he said at last. "What about them?"

The constable raised his shotgun, covering both of us. "Mister," he said slowly, "I'd appreciate it if you'd lay that there rifle aside, easy." Behind us, the high-strung deputy got up from the desk and stepped back. I heard a gun being shakily drawn from its holster.

Jack hesitated a moment, then apparently decided that the man meant what he said, and laid the Sharps across the desk.

"Pick up the gun, Rick, and unlock cell number two," the lawman commanded. "These gents is under arrest for murder."

CHAPTER 9

"You think these are the right ones, Mr. Fowler?" Rick was talking to hide his nervousness. He kept missing the lock with the key.

"They fit the description we got in that telegram from Oakland yesterday," the constable replied. He was standing back just far enough to catch Jack and me both with a double load of buckshot if either of us should make a wrong move. Of course, he would have gotten his deputy too, but I don't think that would have made him hesitate to pull the trigger. "We was warned to look out for a kid, a injun, and a man with a big mule and a mangy little burro. If you see anybody else who answers to that, I sure hope you'll tell me." There was irony in his words, but his voice remained a flat drone.

"Where's the Indian?" asked Rick.

"Likely they parted company somewheres. Anyway, we got part of them."

Jack and I kept silent. The deputy finally succeeded in unlocking the cell door and we went in. It clanged shut behind us.

Fowler leaned his shotgun against the wall and slouched into the leather chair behind the desk. "Mighty obliging of you two to walk right into my office," he said. "Makes my job a sight easier."

"How long you figure to keep us here?" growled Jack.

"Long as I have to. The wire I got from that injun police-man said he'd be passing through in the next couple days. Reckon I can turn you over to him then."

"That's George Crook!" I whispered to Jack.

"Reckon so," he replied, taking off his hat and tossing it onto the narrow iron cot in the darkness at the back of the cell. There was no window in the chamber. The walls were covered with condensed moisture, and things crawled sluggishly between the ancient stones. "It appears he's got more brains than I give him credit for. He must of rode straight to Oakland after crossing the river and sent that wire."

"Shut up in there!" snapped the constable. Then, to his deputy: "Rick, get these gents' animals from the emporium and take them over to the livery stable. Tell Haney he'll be paid out of the town treasury. And tell Otis Ledbetter to get his tail over here on the double. You'll find him in front of the undertaker's parlor. Then go home to your daddy."

Rick said, "Yes, sir," and went out the front door.

"What are we going to do?" I asked Jack. It was dark in the cell, and I could barely make out his outline against the feeble yellow glow of the lamp on the constable's desk fifteen feet away.

"Not a whole lot we can do, except wait," he said. He picked up his hat and stretched out full length on the cot, placing the hat over his eyes. "Meantime, this here's the closest thing I've had to a real bed in near ten years." With that, he lapsed into silence.

I couldn't see how he could be so calm under the circumstances, but I knew he was right. Whatever happened now was out of our hands. The thought didn't cheer me up any.

Jail wasn't as uncomfortable as I'd always imagined it to be. Maybe that was because I'd spent the last four days in the saddle and the last three nights sleeping on the hard ground; I guess the difference between what's good and what's bad depends on what you're comparing it to. About eight feet square, the cell was constructed of the same sturdy stone as the rest of the building, and it had a second cot along the left wall that looked as if it had been added recently to make room for more prisoners. That meant the town was growing.

The only other concession made to comfort was a chipped enamel chamber pot showing underneath the cot.

I tried to get some rest, but it was no use with my nerves as tight as they were, so I settled for sitting on the edge of the cot with my back resting against the damp stone wall. I was still sitting there when the front door opened and the fat old deputy Jack and I had spoken to in front of the undertaker's parlor came into the office. He looked exhausted. His face was shiny with sweat and the barrel of his shotgun was almost dragging on the floor. He nodded to the constable and placed his weapon next to the others in the varnished wooden rack beside the door.

"Where you been, Otis?" asked Fowler. He was seated with his feet propped up on his desk and his hands folded across his stomach. His eyes were closed. I gathered that it had been a long day for both of them.

"Where the hell you think?" the deputy returned. "Over at Jorgenson's, where I been all day, guardin' stiffs. You gone soft in the head or something?"

"I told you to knock off at four o'clock. What you trying to prove, Otis? That you're as good as the rest of the deputies? Hell, there ain't a one of them don't know you're worth more than the whole lot."

Otis took a fresh plug of tobacco from his shirt pocket, picked off all the lint, then cut himself a healthy chew with his jackknife and thrust it into his mouth. "Don't try to slicker me, Bud," he said, chewing. "My eyes ain't half as good as they was five years ago and I wind easy. Last week I went to see Doc Grundy about this pain in my belly; by the time I got to the top of them stairs, I was puffin' like that steamer car that come through here last December. I'm runnin' down fast. But I can still stay on my feet as long as any of them guntotin' young grocery clerks you been pinnin' badges on lately and callin' deputies." He dropped into the wooden captain's chair that faced the desk with a thud that shook the building.

"So why'd you quit?" asked the constable. "Ma Granger show up yet with her brothers?"

"Not yet. I reckon Jorgenson figured he'd grabbed enough free advertisin', 'cause he had the bodies carried inside. I left Sweeney guardin' the door. The others'll likely be checkin' in after they've et."

Fowler nodded. "We got two new prisoners." He jerked his thumb over his shoulder to indicate the cell Jack and I were sharing.

Otis glanced over at us. There was no surprise on his face when he recognized the old man and the boy he had passed the time with while guarding the dead bank robbers earlier. There was just sadness. "What'd they do?" he asked after a moment.

"Murdered a injun policeman over by Quartz Mountain, or so I'm told." The constable rummaged through the papers on top of his desk, found the one he was looking for, and handed it to his deputy. "This come in from Oakland yesterday," he said.

The fat man took a pair of wire-rimmed glasses from a case in his other shirt pocket and put them on to read it. He looked up after a moment. "Who's George Crook?"

Fowler shrugged. "Reckon we'll know that when he gets here."

"Things sure have changed," Otis lamented, returning the wire to the top of the desk. "Time was when we held injuns for whites to pick up."

"Them days is past."

"Yeah." The deputy looked glum for a moment, then his face lit up as if he'd just remembered something. "One thing ain't changed, though," he said. "Effie Ross over at the dry goods says some kid heaved a rock through her front window again last night."

"Not again!" Fowler looked pained.

"Again. I run into her on the way back here, and that's when she told me about it. Says she been tryin' all day to report it, but you're never in the office."

"If she didn't charge such high prices they'd leave her alone." Fowler sighed and got up from behind the desk, picking up his shotgun. "I suppose I ought to go talk to her. Keep an eye on them prisoners till I get back. If this injun Crook comes, make sure you see his warrant afore you let him have them." He took his hat from the peg beside the door and went out.

With an effort, Otis Ledbetter heaved himself out of his chair and stepped around behind the desk. For a moment it looked as if he might come over to speak with me or Jack, then he seemed to think better of it and sank into the constable's chair instead. Rick had left his dime novel on the desk. He picked it up, glanced at the cover, then shrugged and began reading from where the nervous young deputy had left off. Soon the book slid into his lap and his head lolled to one side. In a few minutes he was snoring loudly.

In the adjacent cell, Billy Granger had left his cot and was pacing the stone floor, muttering to himself beneath his breath. A couple of times I caught the words "Ma" and "Ben," and once I heard him mention Crawfordsville, but the rest of it was impossible to make out. He was a skinny kid, as skinny as I was, and he had long blonde hair which, parted in the middle, hung in unruly locks on either side of his high forehead. I say "kid" because he was so much younger than anyone else I'd been in contact with for several days; actually, he was several years older than I was, though he didn't look it. I think his face was what a girl would call handsome, kind of delicate and fair-complexioned, but I can't swear to it because the light in that part of the building was far from good. Also, I'm not a girl.

Jack tried to speak to him once. Lying on the cot with his hat over his face, he turned out not to be asleep as I'd thought, but only resting. He had missed nothing that had happened since the fat deputy entered the office. "Billy," he said quietly, "this here's Jack Butterworth. You probably don't recollect me. I seen you when I was in Kansas. I knowed your pa. We fit together in the war."

There was no answer from the other cell. The young outlaw had stopped pacing when he heard his name, but now he resumed, his boots scraping ceaselessly on stone. Jack didn't try again. Then, ten minutes later: "Mr. Butterworth?"

Jack lifted his hat brim a little. "Yeah, Billy."

Billy was standing still again. His face was a blank shadow. "Pa used to talk about you. A lot. Said you and him was the meanest of all John B. Hood's shock troops."

Jack chuckled softly. "I reckon he was right, Billy. Them was mean times."

"What you want to talk about, Mr. Butterworth?"

"Oh, nothing in particular. Your family maybe. How's your ma and your sister Sharon?"

"I ain't seen Ma in months." Billy's voice was little more than a whisper. "Sharon died last July. Smallpox."

"I'm right sorry to hear that."

"She never was what you call robust. Seems like a week didn't go by but that the doc didn't pay a visit to see how Sharon was gettin' along. Bills piled up pretty regular."

"That why you left home?"

There was a pause. "I guess that was part of it."

"That don't explain why you went with your brothers."

"Man's got to make his livin' somehow."

Jack didn't say anything to that.

"Mr. Butterworth?"

"Yeah, Billy."

"You reckon they'll hang me?"

This time the pause was on Jack's end of the conversation. "I reckon so, Billy."

"But it was Ben fired the shot that killed that old man, not me!" Panic had crept into the young outlaw's voice. "Why do they want to hang me? They already got Ben and Bob and Charlie. Al and Pima Pete had their hands up when they got them. I seen it. Ain't that enough? Why me, too?" He was gripping the bars that separated the two cells in his hands.

"I could answer that, Billy, but you might not like it." Jack had taken off his hat, and now he sat on the edge of his cot, crimping down the brim between his thumb and forefinger.

"Why me?" repeated the other. His voice cracked. He was

closer to hysterics than I'd thought earlier; had been right along, despite his outward calm.

Jack went on crimping his hat as if it were the most important job in the world. "Billy, did you ever tie a tarp down on a wagon?" He must not have expected an answer, because he went on without pausing. "You want to tie down all them corners. If you don't, and leave one of them flapping, first good wind that comes along'll take hold of it and tear the whole sheet off. I reckon that as far as this town is concerned, you're one of them loose corners." He waited to see if Billy had anything to say to that. He didn't. A long silence stretched between them. Jack broke it. "I told you you might not like it."

The last of the Grangers returned to his cot and stretched out with his hands clasped behind his head, staring toward the ceiling. Well, there wasn't much to say after that anyway.

I said to Jack, "You been thinking about how we're going to get out of here?"

He inspected his handiwork on the battered old campaign hat, then put it back on and swung his legs up onto the cot, tilting the brim forward over his face the way he'd had it before. "Thought about it," he said.

"And?"

"Figure we'll get out when they open that door to let us out."

"When will that be?" I asked.

"When George Crook comes to get us."

Something dumped open in the pit of my stomach. "Well," I said quickly, "what about Logan?"

"What about him?"

"Don't you think he'll try to help us?"

"Can't rightly say. Don't know why he'd want to."

I grew angry. "We helped him when he needed us!"

"We had a stake in it then. Can't think why he'd walk into a trap when he can just keep going and save his skin."

I was about to say something else when I heard voices outside the office door. I turned my attention in that direction.

"Let's get out of here," urged one of the voices. "They ain't gonna let nobody see Billy till the trial." It was a young voice, a boy's.

"We can always ask," said another. This one was a little deeper.

They came into the office, a pair of boys in overalls and floppy gray hats faded by the sun and stained with sweat. One, a redhead with a face covered with freckles, looked to be about twelve. The other was a couple of years older and had dark hair and buck teeth. I pegged him right off as a trouble-maker. I hadn't been out of school so long that I didn't know a rowdy when I saw one.

"Hey, it's old Otis," Buck Teeth said. He appeared pleased with this discovery. He led the way up to the desk behind which the old deputy was sleeping and snoring loudly.

"He sure sleeps noisy," commented Freckles.

"My pa says he sleeps all the time when he's supposed to be workin'." Slowly a wicked grin spread over Buck Teeth's face. "Hey, you got a match?"

"Sure, from burnin' trash," said the other.

"Gimme."

The younger boy dug into his right side pocket, came up with a handful of wooden matches, and laid one in his companion's outstretched palm. "What you gonna do?"

"Watch." Buck Teeth struck one of the matches on the edge of the desk. A flame erupted from the red bulb on the end and sizzled loudly. When all the sulphur had burned off, he leaned forward over the desk, and, cupping the match in his hand so that the heat was deflected from his victim's face, he held it under the old deputy's flowing moustache.

Suddenly the chamber pot in our cell clattered across the floor and came up against the bars with a horrendous crash. I jumped at the noise and looked quickly at Jack. He was sitting on the edge of his cot, where he had been when he had hooked his right hand inside the pot and sent it flying. At the same instant, Otis Ledbetter awoke and sprang to his feet with a speed and an agility I would not have thought possible in a man so huge. The boys backed up quickly. Buck Teeth shook out the match.

"What the hell!" exclaimed Otis, confused. Then he saw the burned-out match in the older boy's hand and his face turned cherry red. "Get out of here!" He snatched up the broom that leaned in the corner next to the desk and brandished it like a club. "Git!"

Freckles lit out the door as if the Indians were after him, but Buck Teeth held his ground a moment longer. "I could of burned off all your whiskers and you wouldn't of knowed it, you old tub of lard!"

"Git!" Otis advanced, swinging his makeshift bludgeon. The brat fled. When it was obvious that neither he nor his friend was going to return, the deputy put away the broom and went back to the desk, but not before nodding to Jack. "I'm mighty obliged to you for that warning, friend," he said. They were the first words he'd spoken to either of us since coming into the office. "I've had these here whiskers for forty years; I'd of hated to lose them."

"White hair attracts trouble like an unbranded cow," said Jack.

The fat man sat down heavily in the constable's chair. "I reckon the boy was right, though," he said quietly. "There ain't much use in holdin' onto a deputy who lets kids set fire to him. What if someone was to try and bust Billy, there, out of jail? Likely I'd sleep right through it. Maybe I ought to retire right now."

The front-door handle rattled. Otis spun around in his chair, the color returning to his face. "I thought I told you kids to git!" he shouted.

The door opened and a big man in a leather vest and a broad-brimmed Stetson entered. He had a sixgun strapped to his right hip and a star glittered on his shirt. I recognized him as one of the lawmen who had been helping the fat deputy guard the dead bank robbers earlier. "Back off, Otis," he said joshingly. "I ain't that much younger'n you that you can get away with calling me kid."

"Sweeney, I thought I left you over at Jorgenson's." Otis was obviously upbraiding him to change the subject. He didn't want the younger man to know what had just happened. "Who's watching them stiffs?"

"Nobody. Old Lady Granger and that pair of mooses she calls her brothers showed up to take them back home. I just come back here to check in before I go home. Wife's waiting supper for me. I hope."

"Did Ma say when she'd be comin' in to see Billy?" asked the old deputy.

"She ain't. They loaded them stiffs into their buckboard and took off ten minutes ago." Sweeney dragged out his makings from the fringed pocket of his vest and began building a cigarette.

"She ain't comin'?" It was Billy who spoke. He was on his feet and gripping the bars at the front of his cell. The lamplight painted his face a ghastly yellow.

Sweeney licked his cigarette paper, rolled it, and smoothed it between his fingers. Then he lighted it with a match from his pocket and watched it burn down to the tobacco before he put it to his lips. "Nope. Your name didn't even come up, Billy."

"What'd she say?" Otis wanted to know.

"Nothing." The younger deputy puffed contentedly on his homemade smoke. "Jorgenson claimed she owed him for fixing up Ben, Bob, and Charlie, but she just ignored him. He tried to get me to lock her up. I just smiled. Her brother Josh sort of backed him into a corner and held him there while the other one, Francis I think his name is, wrapped up the bodies in some wet sheets they had with them and stacked them in the wagon like fireplace logs. Then they left. Of course, they didn't take Al and Pima Pete, but I don't think we have to worry much about them. The Grangers is what everybody's interested in."

"She ain't comin'," repeated Billy. This time it was a statement, but I don't think the words had really sunk in yet. He

just stood there and stared out between the bars. He didn't
appear to be looking at anything.

"Well," said Sweeney, "I got a wife and a stew to get back
to, if she's still there and the stew ain't in the dog's belly. Tell
Bud I was here."

With that he turned and breezed out of the office, leaving a
yawning silence behind him. Well, it was *almost* a silence; it
was broken only at ragged intervals by Billy Granger's sub-
dued voice, intoning over and over, "She ain't comin'."

There is something about being in danger that won't let you
give up hope. Jack had been right, of course, when he'd said
that there was no reason to expect Logan to risk his life to
save us; after all, hadn't he come at me with a knife just the
night before? But then I remembered how patient and willing
the Indian had been to treat my horse's wounded thigh when,
armed and in possession of a good mount, he could have left
us both to George Crook's mercy and ridden to safety. Maybe
he would feel that way again. It was a ray of hope, faint
though it was, and I clung to it. I had to. Logan was all we
had.

Meanwhile, it was a good idea to relax. I didn't know what
lay in the near future, and it didn't do any good to wonder
about it. After so many nights sleeping on the rocky ground,
the iron cot was a welcome relief to my aching muscles. I fell
asleep without half trying.

I didn't sleep long, because when I awoke, it was still dark
and Constable Fowler had not yet returned from his meeting
with Effie Ross at the dry goods store. Nevertheless I heard
muffled voices. I sat up and peered through the gloom toward
the amber globe of light that surrounded the kerosene lamp in
the office. Otis Ledbetter, turned halfway around in his chair,
was conversing soberly with another man, whose face I
couldn't see because it was above the lamp's reach. It didn't
matter, though, because I could see the light reflecting off the
shield of metal that the visitor wore pinned to his chest. Once
during the conversation the man standing turned his head to
look at us in the cell, and that's when I saw the gleaming

black hair that fell about his shoulders in the Indian style. They were speaking so low that I couldn't hear a word of what was being said. I didn't have to hear. The Indian had to be George Crook.

"Jack!" I whispered.

"Shhh!" Although he was motionless in his bunk, I could tell that he was watching the scene too. It reminded me of the night he had kept a silent vigil at the window of the old line shack while an intruder prepared to enter our presence; the night we met Logan.

The fat deputy reached into the desk drawer, took out the keys to the cells, and stood up. His voice grew louder as he approached our cell.

"We sure didn't expect you this early, Officer Crook," he said, the keys jingling in his hand. "You must be powerful anxious to get these two back to stand trial." He inserted the key in the lock. As he did so, the Indian came over to join him, crossing through the light to get there. I suppressed a gasp.

The Indian was smiling a funny kind of half-smile that I recognized. I should have. It belonged to Logan.

CHAPTER 10

I don't know if Jack had suspected the identity of the other man before he stepped into the light or if he was as surprised as I was when it turned out to be Logan. If he was, you couldn't tell it by looking at him. His expression remained as wary as if the man wearing the shield were the real George Crook. On the other side of the bars, the Indian kept on smiling and stood back with his rifle leveled at Jack's chest like any conscientious officer of the law who was determined not to give his prisoners any slack. As for me, don't look for my name listed among the actors in my church's next Bible play, because it won't be there. I don't pretend to have talents that aren't mine. That's why I kept my face in shadow so that Otis Ledbetter couldn't read the elation that I am sure was stamped on every feature.

"Out," said the deputy. He swung open the cell door and stepped back to give the Indian a clear field of fire in case anything went wrong. It didn't. We obeyed meekly and stood there with our hands raised over our heads.

"If you can wait till the constable gets back," Ledbetter told Logan, "I'm sure he'll be glad to lend you a couple deputies for the trip back to the reservation."

"That won't be necessary, Deputy," said the bogus policeman. "I can handle these two."

A glint of suspicion dawned in the old lawman's eyes. "Don't make no sense, one man ridin' herd on two criminals. We didn't even do that in the old days, unless there weren't no other way around it."

Logan said, "I've done it before," and motioned to us to

walk ahead of him. We didn't waste any time; Ledbetter's remarks were growing uncomfortable. The Indian nodded to the fat deputy. "Obliged for your help, Mr. Ledbetter. Look me up if you ever get to Idaho." He took a step toward the exit.

"Ain't you forgettin' something?"

We froze. He had remembered the warrant. There was nothing to do now but act. Logan was turning to pull down on him when suddenly he stopped. Nothing happened for a couple of seconds. I sneaked a look.

Otis was holding Jack's buffalo rifle in both hands. "Bud took this from the old man," he said, smiling behind his moustache. "It's a right handsome weapon and I'd sure like to have it, but likely you'll be needing it for evidence." He offered it to the Indian.

Logan covered up his relief by returning the smile. "Thanks," he said, taking charge of the big gun. "Remember what I said about looking me up." He resumed herding us toward the door.

We were halfway there when it opened to reveal Bud Fowler's stout solidness standing on the threshold. His stormy eyes took in first Jack and me planted there with our hands up, then the Indian holding his gun on us, and finally settled on his corpulent second-in-command standing in front of the cells. He had his shotgun in both hands, ready but not threatening.

"You must be George Crook," he said, looking past us at Logan.

The Indian picked up on it quickly. "That's what they call me," he replied after a beat. "I guess that makes you Bud Fowler. Pleased to meet you, Constable. Your name comes up a lot around the council fires of the Nez Percé."

The constable nodded but appeared unmoved by the flattery.

Logan cleared his throat, a little nervously. "Well," he said, "as I told Mr. Ledbetter, Constable, I'm thankful for your efforts. I'll see that the commanding officer at the Lapwai post sends you a letter of citation. Now, if you'll excuse me . . ."

But Fowler held his ground. "Otis, I reckon you got a look at Officer Crook's warrant like I asked you." He looked over in his deputy's direction.

There was a tense silence while the naked question lay where Fowler had dropped it. I heard the watch tick in the pocket of the constable's vest, once, twice. Then everything happened at once. Logan pulled down on Fowler with the Henry in one hand while he threw the Sharps to Jack with the other. In that same instant Jack spun around, caught the big gun, and leveled it at Otis Ledbetter, who was already within three steps of the gun rack beside the door. "Stop right there!" he shouted. His voice sounded like the roar of the Sharps itself in the closeness of the office. The deputy froze. So did Fowler, but by that time he had the shotgun pressed to his hip and his finger was on the trigger. One twitch and you wouldn't have been able to scrape up enough of the three of us to make a decent-sized mince pie.

Logan said, "I know you're too smart to try for two men with that shotgun, Constable."

"Yeah? Try me." The scattergun remained as steady as a rock. If Fowler had rheumatism as his deputy had said, it wasn't present now. His watch ticked once, twice, three times.

"I know you won't," said Logan. "If you do, I'll pull the trigger on you and my friend will do the same on Mr. Ledbetter. You don't want to leave this town without experienced lawmen."

"Lawmen come a nickel a hundred. I'll die if I got to, but I ain't about to turn three murderers loose on Oregon if I can help it. I've knowed Otis enough years to know he feels the same way. Right, Otis?"

"Right, Bud." The deputy's voice was stern. "I'm in for the whole pot."

Tick. Tick. Tick.

Logan said, "If it'll make you feel any better, Constable, we're not murderers. George Crook is. He's the one you'll be turning loose if we die here."

No answer. I had lost interest in everything but the black hollows inside the twin bores of Bud Fowler's shotgun.

Jack said, "Funny thing about killing outlaws, Fowler. Do it twice in one day, town where it happened gets a reputation. Draws trouble. You want somebody like young Rick in charge when that trouble comes?" He kept his attention on Otis, but his voice rang out clearly in the taut stillness.

The speech had an effect on the old lawman. His brain was working behind the stony façade, sifting through Jack's words, separating the wheat from the chaff. Suddenly I knew that everything was going to be all right. He stood his ground a few more moments, but his decision had already been made. He lowered the shotgun.

"Get his gun, Jeff," said Logan.

I put my hand on the shotgun and after a brief resistance Fowler let go of it. I handed it to the Indian.

"I got a fifteen-man police force here," the lawman told him. "You won't get far."

Logan shifted the Henry to his right hand and broke open the captured shotgun with the other. "I'm betting that we will," he said, removing the shells from both barrels and putting them in his pocket. "In any case, Constable, you're out of the game. At least for now." He snapped shut the gun and handed it back to Fowler.

"Speaking of the game," Jack prodded, "it'd be a good idea if we grabbed our winnings and lit out afore George Crook comes to cash our chips in for us."

Logan agreed, and after a little threatening he and Jack succeeded in getting the two peace officers into the vacant cell and locking them in. I glanced at Billy Granger in the adjacent cubicle, half expecting him to try to talk us into taking him along, but he just sat on the edge of his cot and stared at the wall opposite him. He was so preoccupied with his mother's failure to visit him that I don't think he even knew what was going on outside his cell.

"What are we riding?" asked Jack as we were hurrying out.

"Take a look," answered the Indian.

The first sight we saw as we were stepping out the door of the constable's office was that of the four animals tethered to the hitching rail in front. They consisted of a big mule, a dun horse with a white blaze, a spirited mustang, and an over-loaded burro.

Logan said, "My first stop was the livery stable. I got there just as the owner was starting to unload the burro, and that's when he told me that its owner was in jail. He tried to claim that he'd had the animals for three days. I talked him out of that, but I had to pay him for a day's care before he'd turn them over." He pulled the slip knot on the dun's reins and mounted up. Jack and I did the same.

"Where'd you get the money?" Jack wanted to know.

"The same place I got the badge," said the other. "Clyde Pacing Dog had a lot more on him than guns. You never know what might come in handy." He gave his horse a gentle kick and led the way down the street, taking his time so as not to attract attention. I followed his example, but it wasn't easy with my stomach tied up in knots the way it was. I wanted more than anything to gallop. So, for that matter, did the little mustang. I had all I could do to keep it to a brisk trot. Anybody watching us at that moment would have thought that it was just another bunch of drifters pulling out if it weren't for the fact that the man in front and the man in the rear rode with their rifles held ready across the horns of their saddles. Still, nobody bothered us.

Then all hell broke loose.

The front door of the constable's office flew open with a bang and a shotgun bellowed, blasting the darkness with a jet of blinding red flame. A window on the opposite side of the street disintegrated into a thousand pieces. The horses screamed and bolted. There was another roar. Shot skidded past within an inch of my left cheek. I gave the mustang free rein and the lights blossoming in windows on both sides of the street blended into unbroken streaks of yellow as the little stallion broke into a run. I left Jack and Logan clattering along two lengths behind me.

"Did you think to take them keys off of the deputy?" Jack shouted to Logan above the drumming hoofs. cop. 2

"No," shouted the Indian. "Did you think to unload the shotguns in the rack?"

"No."

"I guess that explains it."

We were just drawing abreast of the four-story hotel and restaurant when the double doors opened and the rest of the deputies who had been guarding the dead Grangers earlier poured out into the street, shotguns in hand. One of the original two lawmen—Fowler or Ledbetter, I don't know which—shouted something to them, and then the echo of his words was drowned out in a deafening volley. But by that time we had cleared the last of the street lamps and were galloping through darkness, beyond lethal shotgun range.

After several minutes of hard riding, the mustang regulated its pace to a steady gallop. That's when Jack's mule took advantage of its longer legs to catch up, and we rode abreast like that for a long time, with Logan bringing up the rear on his slower but equally reliable dun. Even the fact that the little burro was still attached to the mule did little to hinder its clean, scooping, long-legged run. Well, this wasn't the first time it had been called upon to pull its master out of a scrape, if there was any truth in the stories Jack told.

"Posse coming," he growled once. I listened, and, after a moment, I heard the faint rumble of pursuing hoofs a quarter mile behind us and coming up fast. "What now?" I asked. My heart was keeping time with my own horse's hoofs.

"Follow me." Jack kicked his mule and it lurched ahead as if the mustang had come to a sudden stop. From then on I was hard put to stay within a half a length of the bigger animal.

At length the ground beneath me changed from the even surface of the road into a grassy bank. From there, it plunged downward at a sharp angle; I had to draw rein hard to keep the mustang from losing its footing and tumbling straight down to the bottom. As it was, we half stumbled, half slid for several hundred feet until the slope leveled out into a shallow basin between ridges that had been left behind when the glaciers carved through Oregon. Thorny bushes raked my legs. Tree branches whipped my face and snatched my hat off my head. At the bottom of the incline, we stopped and waited.

For a long time the only sounds were the panting of our mounts and the whine of mosquitoes homing in on the scent of horse and man just as the buzzards had homed in on the body of Clyde Pacing Dog. Then we heard it. A low rumble like far-off thunder, growing louder as it drew near, and then they were right above us, twenty to thirty men on horseback racing along the high ridge of the road, bridles jingling, coat-tails flapping in the wind of their passage. They seemed to go on and on, and then they were gone, rumbling away into the distance, leaving only clouds of dust swirling black against the scarcely lighter gray of the sky to remind us that they had been there.

The dust had long since settled before anybody made a move. "Let's go," said Jack, and he urged his mule forward across the bowl-shaped dale. Logan and I followed.

The threat of capture was still fresh, and we alternated between galloping and cantering for the next five miles. After that we slowed to a walk to give our mounts a rest. Only then did Jack ask the Indian how he had decided to come to our rescue.

Logan chuckled, a humorless ripple deep in his throat, somewhat like a growl. "When you didn't show up after two hours," he said, "the odds were that something had gone wrong. It didn't take much thought to figure out what it was. That's why I went straight to the livery stable; when someone's arrested, that's where they usually put his horse."

I said, "Why'd you do it? You could have been halfway to Canada by now without us." It was an unnecessary question. I knew why, just as I knew why he had taken the time to treat my bay's wounded thigh. I just wanted to hear it from him.

The Indian's smile was back, mysterious and diabolic. He didn't look at me. "I was getting lonely," he said after a moment. "Besides, I'd kind of like to find out how the buffalo hunt ends up."

"The buffalo hunt!" I laughed. "I'd forgotten all about that."

I turned toward Jack to see if he was smiling too. He wasn't. He hadn't forgotten.

The hours crawled by on the backs of turtles. It was the

first extensive bit of night riding we'd done since the hunt had begun, and I had never realized how much harder it could be than the daylight kind. I tried to calculate how late it was. If I'd only slept for half an hour or so back in the jail, it must have been about nine o'clock when we left. We had probably been riding for at least three hours. Yet we showed no signs of stopping. Despite my short nap, my eyes burned in their sockets and my muscles stung as if I'd been plowing since sunup. Once I nodded off, only to be jerked awake by what I would swear was a deliberate lurch on the part of the double-crossing little mustang. I guess it figured that if it had to stay awake, then so did I. After that I kept alert by making up little dramas wherein we would run out of food out in the middle of nowhere and have to eat the star-faced little troublemaker to stay alive. Pleasant thoughts always make the time pass a little more quickly.

Finally, at what had to be about one o'clock in the morning, we crossed the McKenzie River at a narrow point and camped on the north bank. I didn't realize until I got down from the saddle that I was as hungry as I was sleepy; it had been nearly eighteen hours since we'd last eaten, and for the first time since Jack had told me the story of his lion hunt in Texas, I began to get some idea of how he'd felt after several days without food. Time dragged again while Jack fixed a simple supper of salted beef and potatoes which he baked in their skins at the bottom of the fire. As an added treat he used his knife to open up three of the four cans of peaches he'd purchased in Reuben and handed one to each of us, along with a spoon. I thought it was the most delicious meal I'd had in my life. After days of nothing but beans and bacon, anything had to be an improvement. I've always suspected that the only reason Jack had decided to take along such spare provisions for the first few days was to test my endurance as a camper, because I saw neither another hunk of bacon nor another bean for the rest of the trip.

With my stomach full, the need for sleep returned, and I'm afraid I did little more than go through the motions of washing the plates and utensils in my eagerness to get to bed.

At any rate, when I staggered out of my bedroll before dawn
the next morning, eyes swollen from lack of sleep, the ghost of
last night's beef was crusted around the inside of the skillet in
the form of blackened grease. Jack had to chisel it away with
the point of his knife before he could throw in the slices of
canned ham he had ready to cook. He didn't say a word about
it, but it was painfully obvious that he was making no effort to
conceal my mistake either from myself or from Logan. I made
a mental note right there that, come hell or high water, from
then on I would do nothing else until my duties were completed.

We were riding again by the time the sun showed itself
above the jagged peaks of the Cascade Mountains to our
right. The trail we were following was old and overgrown
with weeds and bunch grass, but its sunken state was evidence that it had seen much use over a long period of time. It
was with something of a shock that I came to realize what
sort of creature had worn that path. Until then I had taken it
for granted that Jack had chosen his erratic pattern of flight to
throw the posse off our track, but I had been wrong. The
reason we had left the road was not merely to elude our pur-
suers, but also to stay with the buffalo run where it wandered
from the beaten track. For Jack Butterworth, the hunt came
before everything else.

I think Logan realized what we were doing at the same
time I did, because he said, "Can't we leave this trail for a
while?"

"Can't track buffalo without tracks," answered Jack. His
eyes searched the ground for signs.

"And while we're tracking buffalo, George Crook's tracking
us." The Indian spoke irritably. His exhaustion was beginning
to tell on his usually unruffled nature. "He's no fool; he knows
we're sticking to this trail by now. He doesn't even have to
work to find us. Let's head up into the mountains."

Jack said nothing.

Logan cursed. "I went along with this buffalo hunt non-
sense because I found it amusing," he said. "I've stopped

laughing. It's time we gave it up and thought about saving ourselves."

"You had your chance to take off," Jack said calmly. "You can still do it, if you've a mind."

"Thanks a lot. You know I need you just as much as you needed me last night."

"Didn't ask for it."

Logan stared at him in disbelief. "Would you rather I'd left you in that cage?"

"Didn't say that."

The Indian fell into a sullen silence. Then he exploded. "Look, we can't hunt and stay ahead of George Crook at the same time!"

"That's true enough," agreed Jack. There was something curious in the way he said it.

"What does that mean?" Logan challenged.

Jack turned a stony face upon his companion. It was the first time he'd looked at either of us all day. "If you're planning to stay ahead of your injun law all the way up to Canada," he said patiently, "you got less brains than I give you credit for. You can't keep running all the time. Sooner or later you got to stop and turn. And it might as well be while we're with you."

"So what's stopping you?" The Indian's tone was half angry, half curious. I don't think he was sure whether or not he was being called a coward.

"You are." When Logan didn't say anything to that, Jack continued. "I ain't running," he explained. "I'm hunting buffalo. When you decide it's time to fight, we'll fight. Till then, we'll hunt. It's up to you."

That ended the conversation. Logan stared at him, his expression thoughtful, but Jack's eyes were already back on the ancient trail. I don't think he remembered a word of what he had just said. But the Indian did.

CHAPTER 11

On May 1, 1898, as any history book will tell you, Commodore Dewey seized control of Manila Bay and sealed the victory of the United States in the Spanish-American War. That, however, is not the reason that date looms so big in my memory. Be patient, and I'll tell you why.

It was the afternoon of the second day after we broke out of the jail in Reuben, and of the sixth after I had first laid eyes on Jack. That morning had found us midway between the towering mountain known as Three Fingered Jack ("No relation," quipped the old hider, with a deadpan expression) and the two mile-high peak of Mount Jefferson in the extreme northeast corner of Linn County. Here we found a huge sink-shaped depression some fifty feet across and nearly eighteen feet deep in the middle of country where there should have been nothing but flat plain. It was full of water, and tall cottonwoods grew along its east shore. It didn't look like something nature would have made, yet it didn't quite resemble anything man had put there either. I asked Jack about it as we were letting our mounts drink the muddy water.

"Buffalo wallow," he said, munching on a dried apple he had taken from his saddlebag. He offered me one, but I shook my head. Logan accepted one and nibbled at it in silence. "Starts as a mud puddle. During shedding season, buffalo scrub around in it to get rid of extra hair and ticks and such. Gets bigger and deeper every year. This here's the biggest I seen yet."

"Bet our buffalo stopped here," I said.

"It did."

I looked at him quickly. His attention was on the ground near where his mule had its front hoofs planted in the water. I followed his gaze. My breath caught in my throat.

The print of a cloven hoof as big as my hand showed deep in the loamy soil at the water's edge. It could not have been more than a day old. "Is that what I think it is?" I asked. My voice was strangely hushed.

"Depends," said Jack. "If you're thinking it belongs to a buffalo, you're right."

Logan snorted. "A track like that could belong to a lot of things. An elk, maybe. Or it might be you're hot on the trail of a stray milk cow."

Jack shook his head. "Elk puts all his weight forward; back of his hoof don't show. And the print's too deep for any ordinary cow or bull. Buffalo carries most of his weight up front. Cow carries hers in back. It's a front hoofprint, and it's deep. Buffalo, all right, and fresh. If we wasn't slowed up in Reuben, we'd of caught him up to his hocks in water." He backed the mule out of the wallow. "Let's see where he come out."

We picked up the beast's trail again on the other side of the depression, a clear path that turned up dirt and left the tall grass bent back in the direction from which it had come. An angry buzz of flies drew our attention to a pile of fresh manure heaped in the middle of the trail. We guided our mounts around it and continued riding. The Indian made no more comments after that.

The trail grew faint as we left the soft earth of the plains and passed into the rocky strata where the mountains had heaved themselves out of the ground ages before, but Jack led the way with the certainty of a man who had lived in the area all his life and knew exactly where he was going. Along about noon, however, our pace began to slow, and finally, in a wooded area near the base of Mount Jefferson, Jack drew up. Logan and I followed suit.

Jack got down and spent a few minutes walking around the area. He took up much of that time studying the ground and the various bushes that grew there, and when he returned to his mule his face wore a puzzled expression.

"Something?" I asked.

"He left the trail," he said. "Headed east, into the mountains."

"Why would he want to do that?" Logan wanted to know.

Jack unslung the canteen from his saddle horn and treated himself to a healthy swallow. "There ain't but one thing would make a buffalo turn off of the run he's following," he said, wiping his mouth with the back of his hand. "And that there's it." He nodded toward the west.

Logan and I looked in that direction. The Indian stiffened and drew his revolver. A group of ten men in sweat-stained hats and bib overalls that had long since faded to a neutral color were advancing through the trees with the measured pace of a party of hunters. They were carrying rifles and shotguns. As they drew near, the apparent leader, a big man with a massive head and a neck like a bull's, raised a thick arm in greeting. I wasn't taken in by this display of friendship. Reaching into my bedroll, I pulled out the reliable Winchester and jacked a shell into the chamber. The noise it made was crisply metallic in the silence of the forest. They pulled up short at the sound.

"Hello, sir," said the leader. He had a funny kind of accent that I couldn't identify at first, but which turned out to be German.

"Howdy," said Jack. His tone was noncommittal. He had freed his Sharps from his saddle scabbard and now he stood holding it casually but ready to use.

The German took off his hat and drew his sleeve across his forehead to clear away the sweat. He had dark hair that looked as if it had been cut with a bowl over his head, and his eyes were hidden beneath the black thatching of his brows. His nose was a knob in the middle of his broad face. I figured him to be about forty years old. "You are maybe having good fortune?" he asked.

"I reckon that depends on what you think we're doing."

Jack's voice remained even, but I noticed his knuckles tighten on the big rifle.

The leader appeared surprised. A look passed between him and the rest of the men in his party. One of them growled something in German. "You are not from Salem?" the leader asked Jack.

"No. Should we be?"

More murmurs. "That is where last week we posted the notices," said the leader. "Are you here for the bounty?"

"Mister, I don't know what you're talking about. Maybe you better start by telling me who you are and what you're doing here with all this iron."

"Iron?" The word puzzled the big German. "*Eisen? Ich nicht verstehe*—I do not understand what you mean by 'iron.' My English, it is not so good yet."

"Guns," said Jack, his impatience showing in his tone. "You got enough firepower here to fight the war twixt the states all over again. What is it, a lynching party?"

"Oh," said the other, and his swarthy face was split by a broad grin of understanding. "Iron; guns. I see. Very colorful. No, sir. This is not, as you say, a lynching party. Honest men do not take the law into their own hands. This much I have learned since coming to this country. No, we are hunting."

"*Buffalo* hunting?" I blurted out. I regretted it immediately, for Jack turned and fixed me with a look that made me shrivel in my saddle.

The German laughed, a booming baritone that echoed loudly in the still woods. "You are having fun with me, young sir. I have been here long enough to know that the magnificent beast of which you speak exists no longer. What we are hunting, sirs, is a dog."

"A dog?" repeated Logan, staring at him from the back of his horse. "Are you sure you don't mean a wolf?"

"No, sir. We have wolves even in my country, and I would not mix them up." The German presented Logan with an expression that was not entirely friendly. We were close to the Warm Springs Indian Reservation, and I suppose he'd had his troubles with the red man before this. He turned toward Jack once again. "It is not an ordinary dog we seek," he explained, "but one that is afflicted with the disease of the brain. He is— how do you say it?—mad." To demonstrate, he bared his teeth and wiggled his fingers in front of his mouth to indicate foaming.

"Hydrophobia?" Jack prompted.

The German nodded vigorously. "Yes, sir. That is it. The fear of water."

Jack said, "I seen some dog tracks on the way here. What's the bounty?"

"One hundred dollars."

I whistled.

"It is a small amount to pay, young sir, for our peace of mind." There was no trace of mirth in the German leader's manner now. "Our women and children have been unable to leave their homes for days. Each morning we find fresh tracks in our yards. Our crops will fail if our families do not help us work them, yet none of us is willing to expose his loved ones to the danger."

"Mad or sane, all animals head for higher ground," said Jack. He gazed off toward the east. "You tried looking for him in the mountains?"

The foreigner looked reluctant. "Many times we have tracked the beast into the mountains, sir. Many times we have turned back. Always his trail is lost among the rocks. No one wishes to continue when he knows not whether he is the hunter or the one who is hunted."

Jack said, "Anything that touches the ground leaves signs. They're hard to find sometimes, but they're there. You just got to know what to look for."

The German's face brightened. "You are a good tracker?"

"I been told that. I usually get what I go after."

"You would consider maybe going after mad dog?"

Jack appeared to think it over. "I might."

The grin returned to the German's face. I stared at Jack

and was on the verge of saying something when Logan put a hand on my arm and silenced me.

"You have our gratitude, sir," said the leader of the Germans, and, turning to his companions, spoke to them rapidly in their own language. Soon they were all smiling. They babbled among themselves and at us like geese in a pen at feeding time. The big man seized Jack's hand in his and pumped it energetically. "I am called Eric Morgenmueller. You will know me as Eric. The names of my friends you will learn in time. It is time we returned to our homes for dinner. I would be honored if you and your young friend would eat at my table." His eyes flickered toward Logan and he added, "The Indian gentleman is also welcome."

The "Indian gentleman" said nothing, but his jaw tightened.

"We'd be right honored to accept," replied Jack reservedly. "I'm Jack Butterworth. The boy's Jeff Curry. The injun calls himself—"

"Sleeping Bow," Logan cut in.

"Sleeping Bow," repeated the other without hesitation. "It appears you got yourself three dog hunters, Mr. Morgenmueller."

"Eric," corrected the German, and he threw his arm around Jack's shoulders as if they had known each other since childhood. The group started walking westward. Logan and I followed on horseback and in silence.

Eric Morgenmueller's spread turned out to be the biggest in the cluster of a dozen or so German-owned farms that occupied the rich territory of northwestern Oregon. It seemed that he and the others had come to America soon after the Franco-Prussian War to escape the inflated taxes imposed on them by Otto von Bismarck after the victory at Sedan. The immigrants had dug into their life savings to buy passage on a wagon train west, and when the government auctioned off several thousand acres that had belonged to a local cattle baron for back taxes they had pooled what was left to purchase the land where their homes now stood. All this we learned from Morgenmueller during the trek to his house. As we drew near, the other members of the hunting party trickled off one by one toward their own dinner tables until we were alone with the big farmer.

Logan and I were dismounting in front of the German's modest two-story dwelling when the screen door opened to a complaining of springs and a woman came out. Jack removed his hat.

"My wife Katerina," said the farmer, indicating the thickset woman with a shy, friendly face and blonde hair done up in odd-looking braids coiled on either side of her head. She wore a white blouse buttoned up to her neck and a black skirt under a flour-streaked white apron. As her husband introduced us, she sank into a deep curtsy, but said nothing. "My wife speaks very little English," the farmer explained. Turning to her again, he said, "*Wo ist Ilse?*"

Katerina Mogenmueller answered him in German and nodded toward the red-painted barn across the yard.

"Ilse!" shouted the big man. "Come out and meet our guests!"

After a moment Ilse appeared from inside the barn and walked toward us with hesitant steps. I confess that I stood and stared at her like the village idiot; in my defense, I can only say that I had good reason.

It was not hard to see that, before age had added lines to her face and inches to her waist, Katerina had once looked much like Ilse. But while the woman was merely pretty, the girl was beautiful in a way that the farmer's wife could never have been; and, while Katerina's hair was corn-yellow, Ilse's was as blindingly blonde as a ripe field of wheat under a bright sun. They resembled each other in hair style and dress, but other than that there was no longer any comparison between the two. The girl looked to be about seventeen.

"Yes, Papa?" she said when she had joined Morgenmueller in front of the house. Her crisp blue eyes flickered over the group of strange men who stood in her yard. I thought they lingered on me for an instant, but don't go trusting my judg-

ment too much because I was in love. I will state definitely
that she blushed ever so slightly.

The big farmer told her our names, after which she did a
graceful imitation of her mother's Old World curtsy. As she
came back up, I noticed the fine dust of freckles at the tops of
her cheeks. "I am very pleased to meet you, sirs," she said,
with just a trace of an accent.

"Ilse, see that Herman unsaddles and feeds our guests'
horses. They are staying for dinner." Morgenmueller shooed
his wife into the house and motioned for us to follow. He
came last. As the screen door closed, I caught a glimpse of
Ilse helping a lanky, sullen-looking young man lead our
mounts toward the barn. Why is it that other people's farm
hands always seem to be so at odds with the rest of the
world? Or was I just jealous?

The ground floor of the farmer's house was taken up by a
single room that served both as parlor and kitchen, with a
square linen-covered table standing in between to designate
the dining area. A carved wooden crucifix hung on the wall
above the stone fireplace. Lace doilies decorated the simple
upholstered chairs and the tired-looking sofa, and an oaken
buffet in the corner sported a scarf embroidered in many
colors on its top. In one of the chairs sat an old lady in a black
lace dress fastened at her neck with a big turquoise brooch.
Her face was smooth and her gray hair was streaked with
white. She regarded Jack with interest.

"Gretchen Steiner, my wife's mother," Morgenmueller told
us. "She speaks no English at all." He introduced us to her in
rapid German.

She smiled, nodded, said *Guten Tag*—and all the time she
kept her bright little eyes riveted on Jack. He nodded to her a
little uncomfortably. At this, Logan smiled for the first time
since we had met the hunting party out in the woods.

"And now, gentlemen," said the head of the household, "a
race. The first man to reach the washbasin receives the
benefits of clean water."

"Eric!" chided his wife. "*Still!*" She turned to us. "My hus-

band, he is joking always, sirs. Clean water you will find much
of on the back porch."

During dinner, which turned out to be a thoroughly American assortment involving two roast ducks with dressing, a
salad, biscuits, mashed potatoes, beans, asparagus, and a fresh
rhubarb pie for dessert, Eric Morgenmueller revealed that for
a little while he had served in the Army of Prussia. That set
the tone of the conversation, and for the next twenty minutes
he and Jack swapped war stories that grew steadily more
outlandish and unbelievable as the meal progressed. Nevertheless the talk was not without its controls. Every time the
farmer touched on a subject that did not seem fitting for
polite company, his wife would clear her throat loudly, and
without an instant's hesitation he would veer off onto a
different track. This had a tempering effect on Jack as well.
Most of the tales he related dealt with humorous incidents that
had taken place between battles. The upshot of it was that the
rest of the diners were forced to sit and suffer through some of
the dullest war stories that had ever been told.

Logan bore his part of the burden in silence. I think he was
still disturbed over having been called an "Indian gentleman"
and considered apart from the rest of us, but that he was also
a little surprised that he had been invited to this table at all.
He wasn't the only one who was disconcerted by his position.
Even Jack had trouble concentrating either on his conversation or on his meal, because every time he looked up from
his plate, he saw Frau Steiner watching him from her place
across the table with the eye of a shopper weighing in her
mind the merits of the item she is considering buying. As for
me, I don't think I tasted a bite of what must have been a delicious meal because of the constant realization that pretty
Ilse Morgenmueller was sitting at my left elbow. She smelled
of lemon verbena, and to this day I can't come into contact
with that sweet aroma without thinking of that meal. I expect
it affected the flavor of the duck I was eating as well.

Once Ilse said something to her mother across the corner of
the table in German, and her father disengaged himself from

his conversation with Jack to stare at her in disapproval. "Ilse," he said, "I have raised you better than this. You know that it is not polite to speak in the language of our home when we have guests at table who do not understand."

The girl lowered her eyes. "I am sorry, Papa."

"That is not good enough," he said sternly. "Now you must repeat what you said in English so that our guests may hear."

She reddened. "Papa, I cannot!"

The farmer's brow grew dark. "Is this how you obey your father? Do what I have told you to do! Ilse!"

She was looking down at her plate. Her face was bright red and tears glistened on her long eyelashes. The silence after her father's harsh words hung heavy in the room.

"Very well, Papa, if you insist." It was Katerina Morgenmueller who had spoken. Her daughter turned a pleading face on her and shook her head, but the woman laid her work-roughened hand on Ilse's slender white one atop the table and gave it a reassuring squeeze. She looked at her husband. "Since you must know," she said, "Ilse was asking me if I did not think the American boy was very handsome."

Morgenmueller looked as if someone had struck him in the face with the barn door. Jack eyed me curiously, but no real change came over his normally placid features. Logan suppressed a smile. Frau Steiner glanced from face to face, trying to learn from them what she could not from the words that had passed between her daughter and her son-in-law. Ilse stared at her plate as if trying to see through it to the table. Her mother tightened her grip on her little hand. I suppose I should say I was as embarrassed as she was, that I hadn't felt this way since the time the teacher intercepted the love note I had been passing to Gail Donaghue in the first row and read it aloud to the class, but it wasn't true. Not entirely. I was red-faced, sure, but the thought that someone like Ilse could consider a scrawny scarecrow like me handsome made the sting unimportant. The only shadow was the way it had affected the girl at my side.

But Ilse's mother was not finished. "You broke in, Papa, before I could answer the question." She looked at me and smiled. "Yes, Ilse, I do think he is very handsome. A bit too thin, perhaps, but, *Himmel!* We cannot have everything."

She was still looking in my direction. I knew what was expected of me. "Thank you, Ilse," I said, rising to the occasion. The girl kept her head down, but I saw that she was watching me out of the corner of her eye. "I think you are very pretty."

"*Ja.* Well." The farmer had recovered from his shock. "We will talk no more of this." Immediately he resumed his conversation with Jack from the point where he had left off, but not before Ilse favored me with a shy but grateful smile. It was soon gone, but it was enough to get me through the rest of the meal with the feeling that I had done something Sir Galahad would have been proud of had he seen it.

When dinner was over, Jack complimented Mrs. Morgenmueller on the food and pushed his plate aside so that he could lay his forearms before him on the table. "Let's hear some about this here mad dog."

Morgenmueller was in the midst of filling his pipe, a charred briar with a curved stem, from a can of tobacco he kept within easy reach atop a cabinet near the table. He frowned. "It is what you would call a mongrel," he said, speaking through clenched teeth as he lit the pipe. A cloud of blue smoke drifted across the table. "We are thinking it belonged to someone in Cascadia, and that it was turned loose because it was too big and ate too much. It has been wandering about the settlement for the last year, begging scraps of food in the daytime and sleeping under porches at night. Everyone in the settlement has given it *Imbisse*—handouts—at one time or another. It was always a friendly dog. Even the children played with it when they were not in school or at work in the fields.

"Then, early last month, Alfred Schumann next door shot a skunk that killed one of his wife's chickens in broad daylight. Two weeks later, Schumann's young son Fritz was playing in his back yard when the dog slunk out of the bushes and stood there staring at him. It is a big yellow animal, shaggy, and

marked by a foot-long scar along its right side. Fritz went
over to pet it, but it started growling and he stopped. Just
then Schumann came back from plowing. The dog was just
beginning to foam at the mouth. He ran inside the house, took
down his shotgun, and fired at the dog, but he was afraid of
hitting his son and he missed. The dog yelped and ran away.
Since then it has been seen almost every day, and shot at several times, but always it returns. We are thinking that the
skunk Schumann shot was rabid, and that it must have bitten
the dog. We do not wish to have the same thing happen to
our children, Herr Butterworth. Hence the one-hundred-dollar
bounty." He puffed on his pipe.

"Who got bit?" asked Jack.

The German took his pipe out of his mouth and stared at
him in surprise. "How did you know?"

Jack said, "I heared a lot of stories in my time. I know when
something's left out."

"I see," said the farmer. He clamped the stem between his
teeth and rose from the table. "Come with me, sirs."

He led us to a corncrib that stood on the other side of the
barn, a long building with a slanted roof and walls made of
slats nailed an inch apart from each other to allow plenty of
light to enter. I heard a snarling sound as we approached, and
wondered with a twinge of fear if the dog were inside. I was
sure Morgenmueller heard it too, but it didn't slow him down
any as he took a key out of his pocket and sprang the steel
padlock that kept the door shut. He swung it open and
stepped aside to let us enter.

I went inside first—and backed up so fast that I bumped
into Jack, who was coming in behind me. At the far end of the
building, chained to one of the four stout beams that supported the roof, a balding, middle-aged man strained at his
shackles and stared wildly at us, snarling and snapping like a
captured wolf. His plaid shirt was shredded and soaked with
sweat, his blue jeans covered with old corn silk from scrubbing around on the shuck-littered dirt floor. Thick saliva
formed at the corners of his mouth and dripped grotesquely

onto the front of his shirt. The building shook with his exertions.

"Rufus Brinker," intoned Morgenmueller, in a flat voice. "Until last week, he was the best hand I've had ever. He was fixing a fence in the potato patch when he saw the dog on the other side and jumped over to try and hit it with his axe. He missed and it bit him on the wrist. He did not bother to tell us about it for days. By that time it was too late to do anything about it. He has been like this since Monday."

"Can't anything be done for him?" I asked. I stared in morbid fascination at the thing that had once been a man but which was now nothing more than a wild animal.

The German shook his head. "I have seen this happen in my country, where bats carry the dread disease from place to place. His breathing muscles, they will work with more and more difficulty, and finally they will cease to function. Then he will die. All we can do is keep him in chains so that he does not infect others."

Jack said, "The dog's better off. Him we can shoot."

Morgenmueller nodded agreement. "The law is a strange thing, sirs," he said. "It protects a man from everything but himself."

"Let's go hunting," said Jack.

The first chance I had to speak to Jack alone came when he, Logan, and I separated ourselves from the rest of the hunters to head up the mountain. We were on foot. This, the hider explained, was to eliminate the possibility of our mounts panicking at the sight of the hunted beast and throwing us straight into its jaws. Each of us had his rifle in hand.

"Why are we doing this?" I asked. "Seems to me there are better ways to pay for a meal, ways that won't take up so much of our valuable time."

Jack paused to inspect a possible sign on the barren ground at his feet, then continued leading the way up the steep grade that wound around the mountain. "We got to go this way anyway," he replied. "And we might as well do it for a hundred dollars as for hide and meat."

"Since when do you care so much about money?" I challenged.

"Since I used the last of it to pay for our grub back in Reuben."

"I have money."

"I don't." That was the end of the conversation.

To Logan, I said, "How did you come up with a name like Sleeping Bow? It sounds like something out of a dime novel."

He shrugged. "I can't help that. It's my real name."

I wanted to delve deeper into that mystery, but we had come to a flat expanse of ground covered with green bushes and tall poplars, and Jack signaled to us to spread out and advance through it much as John B. Hood's infantry must have done when combing the countryside for Yankee stragglers. The foliage grew thicker as we strode forward, and soon the others were out of sight beyond a clump of trees. That's when I heard something moving in the brush thirty feet to the right of me.

I stopped. The leaves were still rattling where they had been disturbed. I stood waiting, my rifle aimed toward the bushes. My heart pounded. There was a prolonged period during which I heard nothing but the wind moving sluggishly through the treetops, and I began to think that whatever it was had gone away. I lowered the rifle.

Then the bushes shook again and George Crook stepped out into the open.

CHAPTER 12

He was leading a paint pony by its regulation U. S. Army bridle when he emerged from the bushes. A spare man, leaner than Logan though not so lean as Jack, he wore a Sam Browne belt strapped over a hip-length military jacket of a light brownish color and carried an 1895 lever-action Winchester carbine in his right hand. The butt of an army revolver showed above the top of his holster. His hair was long and black like Logan's, but unlike Logan's it was topped with a tall-crowned hat of the same color as his jacket with a wide flat brim and four egg-shaped dents around the top. I was not to learn until much later that this was the official uniform of the men who were fighting for the United States in Cuba, and that George Crook had somehow gotten hold of it before it was even issued to the soldiers at the Lapwai army post. Under the jacket his chest was bare.

You'll know him by his twisted face, Logan had said, but it wasn't until he stepped into the sunlight that I realized the two sides of the Indian's face didn't match. In putting him back together after the mishap with the four sticks of dynamite, his doctors had failed to properly line up his features, with the result that the right half of his face was cocked a full half an inch lower than the left. His right eye, cheekbone, and even the right side of his mouth existed on a different plane from that of their mates on the other side of his nose. This irregularity, while far from horrible, made for an uneven countenance that was as sinister as it was disturbing. I confess that for at least a full minute after he stepped into the clearing I did nothing but stand and stare at him.

I reckon he was used to that reaction by now, though, because instead of demanding to know what I was gaping at, he just smiled. That is, he *tried* to smile, but the best he could manage was an upward twist of the left side of his mouth while the other half remained motionless. It came home to me then that that whole section of his face was dead, and that all he could ever hope to accomplish with the good side was a grotesque parody of intelligent expression.

"Howdy," he said. His voice was neither shrill nor deep, but halfway in between, and tainted with a slight western twang.

I said nothing. I was in such a state that he could have walked up and taken my rifle away from me without any danger of my pulling the trigger. No such thought occurred to him, however, and his next words came as such a surprise that I forgot my shock as their full meaning became clear.

"I'm looking for two men," he told me. "An Indian and an old man. They got a boy with them too, about your age or maybe a little younger. Old man rides a mule. Maybe you seen someone who answers to that."

It slowly dawned on me that he had no idea who I was. He'd never seen me up close before, and now, finding me out here alone and apparently running away from no one, he had obviously assumed that I was one of the settlers who lived in the area. I wasn't about to let him think otherwise. Thinking quickly, I fell back on a phrase I'd heard one of the German farmers use earlier when Jack had tried to strike up a conversation with him. "*Ich spreche kein Englisch,*" I said, in as thick a European accent as I could muster.

Irritation flickered over the good side of his face. "Three people," he said slowly, letting go of his pony's bridle to hold up three fingers. "An Indian, an old man, and a boy." He used those same fingers to indicate first feathers at the back of his head like an Indian might wear, then lines of age on his face, and finally to describe a person of short stature, such as a child. I didn't much like that, being as tall as he was, but I composed my face into a blank expression to let him know that I didn't understand what he was talking about.

"*Ich spreche kein Englisch,*" I repeated.

"Bah!" He turned his back on me and mounted the paint. I saw then that, in addition to the rifle he carried and the gun he wore on his hip, he also had a Colt Peacemaker thrust into a scabbard near the front of the saddle. "Stupid goddamn foreigners," he muttered, and spurred the pony forward down the slope. It was only then that I noticed he *was* wearing spurs—the big Mexican kind with spiked rowels which, used wrong, could scar a horse's flanks for life. I had always thought that no Indian would be caught dead wearing them.

I suppose I should at least have given some thought about shooting him as he picked his way down the grade, but I didn't. Even if I had, I would not have done so. To me, a man who would shoot another man in the back is the blackest villain that walks God's good earth, and there is nothing you can say about self-preservation that will change my mind on that score. I have no wish to go down in history with the dirty little coward who shot Mr. Howard. Anyway, I stood there watching him until his pony's little black and white rump disappeared among the trees that clustered around the bottom of the mountain, and then I hightailed it to find Jack and Logan.

"Did he say where he was going?" asked Jack after I had breathlessly spilled out my story to them on the other side of the copse of trees that had separated us.

I shook my head. I was out of breath and my chest was heaving.

Logan looked angry. I would have expected him to look scared, but he didn't. He turned on Jack, fists clenched around his rifle. "Are you satisfied?" he demanded. "Now you've landed us right in his lap!"

"What do we do now?" I asked Jack between gasps for air.

"Keep hunting, I reckon." He took his rifle in both hands and resumed the long climb to the top of the mountain.

"And what will we do when we get back and find George Crook waiting for us?" asked Logan belligerently, falling into step beside him. I followed at a pace that would allow me to catch my breath.

"He won't be."

"How can you be so sure?"

"Ain't never sure about nothing," said Jack. "But the injun's too smart to jump us with witnesses around."

"That didn't seem to bother him where Sam Dailey was concerned," argued the Indian.

"And because of that he's chased you across three states. He won't make that mistake again. No, he'll bide his time till we're alone with nobody else around. Then he'll swoop down on us like a hawk on a chicken the minute the farmer leaves the barnyard."

"Like now," said Logan.

Jack shook his head. "He don't know we're here yet. Give him time."

Once we found a clear set of paw prints in the soft alluvium that had washed down from the top of the mountain, but these were two days old at least and there were no fresh signs that the dog had been in the area since then. From there we took a path down on the other side and followed it through thick undergrowth to a pocket between the peaks, where we stopped to rest. You hear a lot about the oases of the Sahara, but I can tell you right now that you will never find a spot more beautiful than the one we stumbled upon by accident in the northern part of the Cascade Range. Below us, its shores ringed by pines that stretched as high as two hundred feet into the cloud-sprinkled sky, a broad blue lake with a surface like a polished mirror curved lazily westward around the rocky base of the mountain we had just crossed. Beyond it, to the north, where clouds enshrouded its jagged summit, a waterfall white with the rage of its torrent spilled over the top of a fluted wall of rock and plunged six hundred feet straight down to a boiling inlet from which the lake was fed. Here the water crashed and gurgled over a jumble of angular rocks until, tamed at last, it wandered dazedly into the placid waters beyond the grotto. Even from a distance of a quarter of a mile, which was as close as we could get to it without actually swimming the lake, the roar of the falls was deafening.

"That must be the Shoshone Falls Morgenmueller told us about," Logan observed. Even though he was shouting at the top of his lungs, his words were nearly drowned out by the rushing water.

Jack took a swig from his canteen and handed it to the Indian. "There's a falls like this in Montana," he shouted. "Friend of mine was driving a wagonload of hides along the bank upriver when it hit a rock and tipped over, horses and all. All we found at the bottom was a tattered hide and a bunch of splinters."

"Don't any of your friends die of natural causes?" asked Logan.

"Depends on what you call natural," said Jack.

An hour before sundown we came across a trail of dog tracks on the south face of Mount Jefferson that were so fresh I swear they were still warm. "Weather's cooling," said Jack. "He's headed back down to the settlement."

The trail became easier to read as we left the rocks and started across the softer soil at ground level. Here trees and bushes of every description threw long shadows across the ground and made it seem as if we were advancing through a dark tunnel. Our pace slowed considerably.

"Ease up." Jack's voice had dropped to a whisper. "He knows we're trailing him."

It was dusk, when the pale half-moon shared the sky with the waning sun and every shadow carried a menace of its own. I became acutely conscious of every sound beyond that of our boots slithering through the dew-dampened grass. Crickets chirped, then fell silent as we drew near them. Two miles behind us the waterfall was a steady but muted roar. Other than that it was still.

Suddenly the air rang with a bellow of animal fury, and, eyes blazing in the red sunlight, jaws horribly agape, a four-legged monster came galloping straight toward us through the aisle formed by the surrounding trees. For a crucial instant I froze and so did Logan. But Jack lifted his Sharps to his shoulder and fired just as the dog was leaping for his throat. The bawling roar changed into a shriek, the animal exploded six feet backwards in a cloud of smoke and blood, and dropped, a lifeless, broken thing, to the ground. It was all over in less than a second.

For a long time we stood over the twisted form lying in a litter of its own guts and nobody said a word. The stink of spent gunpowder hung like a dirty shirt over the entire scene. Finally Jack spelled out the dead creature's epitaph.

"He made somebody a good dog once," was all he said.

We were still a good half mile from Morgenmueller's house when the word spread that we were bringing the mad dog in dead, and farmers and their families began to crowd around us, bombarding us with questions in mile-a-minute German. We had used the length of rope Jack had brought with him to lash the bloody corpse to a tree limb, and now Logan and I carried it between us while Jack cleared the way ahead. The dog's head bounced with each step and dripped blood and foam from its grinning mouth.

Morgenmueller must have heard the commotion, because when we got to his place the front door opened and threw a shaft of light across the yard and he stepped out to meet us. He hadn't beaten us back by much; he was still wearing his knee-length Prussian army boots and canvas hunting jacket. Ilse appeared in the doorway, but he waved her back into the house. "I heard the shot as I was coming in," he said, once he was sure his daughter had pushed the door shut with her inside. It stayed open a crack, but I didn't bring this to the farmer's attention. He bent down to examine the dead animal. "*Ja.* That is him." He straightened. "You had trouble?" His eyes were on Jack's shirt front. In the light coming from inside the house I noticed for the first time that the buckskin was spattered with blood.

"Dog's blood," Jack assured him. "Not mine."

"It could be no other," said the farmer. Nevertheless he looked relieved. He barked something in German to two of his neighbors standing nearby, after which they moved in and took the dog from Logan and me. Carrying it between them, they tramped around the corner of the house.

"Make sure they burn that there corpse," said Jack.

"Such will be done." Morgenmueller regarded him with admiration. "You have earned more than a hundred dollars this day, Herr Butterworth," he told him. "You have earned also the respect and gratitude of this settlement. I insist that to-night you will sleep beneath my roof."

Jack cast a sideways glance at Logan, where their gazes met, then shook his head. "I thank you kindly, Eric," he said, "but we got a schedule to keep. I reckon we'll just be moving on."

The German looked disappointed for a moment, but then his face brightened. "As you wish, sir. But I would be a traitor to my faith if I allowed you to leave without supper. Do not argue with me on this, because my mind, it is made up."

"Well, when you put it that way, I reckon I can't rightly refuse," said the hider.

"*Schön gut*. I will have Katerina bring to you a clean shirt as you wash."

Jack said, "That won't be necessary."

"But it is no trouble," argued the other.

"You don't rightly understand." Jack pulled out the blood-stained front of his shirt and frowned at it. "This shirt and me, we been together near fifteen years. If it's all the same to you, I'll just give it a scrubbing and put it back on."

"And what will you wear while it dries? Come, my friend; allow me to lend you one of my shirts, if only for a little while."

Jack's reply was tolerant but firm. "Like I told the boy, you got to let buckskin dry on your body or you'll never wear it again. I'm obliged to you for the offer, but it just ain't necessary."

The farmer shrugged. "As you wish," he said defeatedly. "But I must advise you to be very careful when you wash the garment. The blood of the mad dog, it can be as dangerous as his bite if it is allowed to penetrate the skin."

"It'll have to get through thirty years' worth of calluses first," said Jack.

Steam was rising from the pitcher of hot water Katerina Morgenmueller had left for Jack's use on the back porch when we got there. He poured some of it into the basin and pulled his shirt off over his head. The sight of Jack Butterworth without his shirt on was not one you'd be likely to forget. Lean and corded, his torso was a map of old scars, some of which were as big and as blue as the weals that were left on his mule after it had tangled with the grizzly. At least one of them, now a healed-over semicircle about two inches below his heart, was unquestionably the mark of a bullet. It must have been less than a memory to him now, but at one time the wound that had made it had nearly cost him his life. It was one thing to shrug off Jack's stories as exaggerations when he was telling them; it was quite another to do so when faced, as I was at that moment, with the hard evidence that the events he reported had indeed taken place.

I wasn't the only one who was fascinated by the spectacle. When I looked over at Logan leaning against the porch railing, I saw that he was staring at him too, and with a wide-eyed wonder that drew Jack's attention when he finished washing his face and looked up from the clean towel he had used to dry off. "What're you looking at?"

"I'm not sure," the Indian replied. "It looks like a battlefield."

Nothing more was said about it. Jack crumpled his shirt into the basin and began kneading it. The water took on a pinkish tint.

Logan left the railing. "I'll check on the horses," he said, and started walking toward the barn.

"I'll go with you," I said.

That seemed to surprise him. He stopped and half-turned, fixing me with a suspicious expression. "Keeping an eye on me?" His tone was accusing.

"No," I retorted, meeting his gaze. "Should I?"

"That depends." His back was toward me and he was crossing the yard in healthy strides. "If you think you have to, you
have to."

I fell into step beside him, carrying my Winchester. I was
never without it these days. "I just wanted to talk. Is there
anything wrong with that?"

"What do you want to talk about?" He pulled open the big
barn door and led the way into the silence inside. Morgenmueller had left a lantern burning for us on a nail beside the
door. Its uneven yellow glow created a protective womb of
light that kept the shadows in the building's corners at bay.

"Things," I said, and hauled myself up into a sitting position
atop the stall that was occupied by Logan's dun. I heard
Jack's mule shuffling around in its assigned place next to it,
and once my mustang gave the side of its stall a kick so that
I'd be sure to notice it. The burro's jaws munched resignedly
at a mouthful of oats in the stall across the way. "Why did
you say that your real name is Sleeping Bow?"

I was hoping that by springing the question on him suddenly I'd catch him off his guard, but it didn't work. His
movements remained casual as he squatted beside the dun
and lifted its right front hoof. "That's because it is," he answered calmly. He used his knife to pare away the hoof where
it had grown over the shoe. Unlike George Crook, his late
partner had ridden a shod pony.

"I still don't understand."

The scraping sound continued for several seconds before he
went on. "Among the Indians," he explained, inspecting his
work, "one has two names during the course of his life; the
one he is given by his parents and the one he earns when he is
older. My father was a man of action. He named me Sleeping
Bow in a fit of bitterness because when I slept, which was
often, he thought I resembled an unstrung bow, limp and useless. Finally he decided to do something about my laziness.
On my tenth birthday he handed me a knife and told me to go

out and bring back some game. I was not to come back, he said, until I had something to show him."

He paused to brush the scrapings from his jeans, then continued. "I'm not as good a storyteller as Jack, so I won't go into details." His knife struck sparks against the steel shoe. "But when I returned to the hut three days later, grimy and covered with blood, I dragged behind me a buck deer that weighed in at a hundred pounds on Sam Dailey's meat scale. That's when my father told me to choose whatever name I wished to be called." He let go of the horse's hoof and stood up.

"But why Logan?" I asked. "Why not an Indian name?"

"John Logan was the Christian name taken by a Cayuga Indian chief in Pennsylvania during the last century," he said, smiling cryptically. "Four years after he moved to the Ohio River, his family was murdered by a gang of white renegades at Yellow Creek. Logan is said to have personally taken thirty scalps before his revenge was cut short by a drunken brawl that ended in his death."

I made a face. "It seems to me you could choose a better namesake than a drunk and a murderer," I said.

The smile remained. "You could be right," he replied. "Perhaps my choice was colored by the fact that my father died of pneumonia in a white man's prison before I could decide what name to take."

His words had little time to sink in, because scarcely had he finished delivering them when a shot exploded outside the barn. It was followed immediately by a second, and then there was an awful wrenching sound, as of a door being torn from its hinges. Logan was running after the first report. It took me a little longer to react, but I was right behind him before the second had died away.

The night was a mass of confusion. Jack, his wet shirt flapping outside his pants, had tipped over the washbasin in his haste to get to the corncrib behind the barn, where the shots had originated, and was now eating up the distance between the house and the rickety little building in long-legged strides.

He had his Sharps with him. The back door of the house banged open and Eric Morgenmueller came running out carrying the old-fashioned fowling piece he had used in hunting the mad dog earlier. I caught a glimpse of his wife standing in the doorway and of Ilse standing behind her, and then I stopped watching and took off in the others' footsteps. I shifted my Winchester to a two-handed grip, for I had no idea what I was racing into.

There was enough moonlight for me to see the door of the corncrib as I rounded the barn, or at least to see where it should have been, because the door was no longer there. In its place was a gaping black hole. This came as no surprise; I had already determined that the wrenching sound I had heard was that of the door being ripped loose. But that didn't stop a chill from overtaking me when I saw that my suspicions were right. I knew what that missing door meant.

"He's loose!" Herman, the sullen young farm hand, came running out of the corncrib, a lighted lantern dangling from his hand.

"There he is!" Logan, who had reached the building two steps behind Herman, raised his Henry and fired away off to my right. Fire streaked out of the barrel. The report was answered almost simultaneously by a howl of brute anguish mixed with fury. I turned toward its source—and then something clubbed me hard on the right temple and I went down in a swirl of red fire and popping blue lights. Something vaulted over me with a grunt, something hot and wet splattered onto my face. I wondered confusedly if it were my blood, and if I'd been shot. There were more shots, but they were too rapid, fired in frantic haste and with little hope of hitting their target. Jack's Sharps boomed once. I rolled over groggily, just in time to see a flash of plaid shirt in the moonlight as the thing that had knocked me down came loping back in my direction. Rufus Brinker's breath heaved painfully in and out of his diseased lungs. I drew a bead on the plaid shirt with my Winchester, and, just as he leaped over me for the second time, fired. He gasped and came down knee-first on my stomach, knocking the wind out of me. A length of chain fell across my face. Then he was up again and stumbling off into the night. I hoisted myself up onto one knee and snapped off three more shots, but by that time he was out of sight and I was only throwing lead into a black void. I climbed unsteadily to my feet.

"You all right?" It was Logan. He had been running to my aid when the madman had gotten up and made his final dash for freedom. A plume of smoke twisted out of the barrel of his rifle.

"I think so," I said. I put a hand to the side of my head and it came back dry. That was a relief. The blood that had splashed on my face had not been mine. "What happened?"

"Someone turned Rufus Brinker loose," said the Indian.

Herman came by, studying the ground within the circle of light shed by his lantern. "He has been hit once at least," he informed us. "There is much blood here."

"Are you sure he didn't escape on his own?" I asked Logan.

"We'll know soon enough. Let me have that lantern." He held out his hand to Herman, who turned over the light, then led the way toward the open corncrib. The rest of us followed. Jack and Morgenmueller brought up the rear.

Inside the building, the lantern threw weird shadows across the slat walls as Logan held it up to show us the post to which the madman had been chained. The rust-colored iron staple that had secured his manacles was broken and twisted. The metal shone dully at the fresh break.

"That explains the shots," Logan said. "He must have slid his rifle in between the slats and aimed at the moonlight showing on the staple. It took him two shots, but it's a thick piece of metal. Rufus did the rest."

"But, why?" Morgenmueller's face was a study in astonishment. "Who would do something like this?"

The Indian looked over at Jack. "Are you a betting man?" he inquired.

"Not on this," said the other, shaking his head.

The German farmer glanced from one face to the other.

"*Was ist los?*" he asked sharply. "There is maybe something I should know?"

There was a pause, during which Logan and Jack exchanged glances. Jack nodded. The Indian seemed to be about to speak when a scream pierced the silence.

"Katerina! *Mein Gott!*" Morgenmueller forced his way past Jack and took off at a run toward the house. He was vaulting over the threshold of the back door by the time the rest of us rounded the barn.

We found Katerina Morgenmueller on her knees on the floor of the living room, administering to her mother, who was stretched full length across the faded rug. She was sobbing hysterically. Two of the upholstered chairs had been overturned. Her husband stood over the scene, fowling piece in hand and a scared look on his face. "What has happened?" he demanded. "Where is Ilse?"

"He took her." Katerina's voice was shrill. "He came in the front door and took her. *Mutter* tried to stop him. He hit her with his rifle." She burst into tears and rocked back and forth with *Frau* Steiner's head in her lap. The older woman began to moan faintly.

"Who took her? Rufus?" Morgenmueller's face was dead white.

His wife shook her head frantically. "He was an Indian. His face—it was *schrecklich*—horrible. He grabbed Ilse and hit *Mutter* and went out the front door."

"Did he say anything?" It was Logan who spoke.

"He—he said to tell someone named Logan that he would be waiting for him in the mountains. I did not understand what he meant. He said Logan would know."

"Logan?" said the farmer. "Who is Logan?"

The Indian didn't answer him. He spun on his heel and began striding toward the back door.

"Where you going?" asked Jack.

"For ammunition." Logan was already outside and halfway to the barn. He raised his voice. "You were right. It's time to stop and turn."

CHAPTER 13

The right thing for me to have done, of course, would have been to try to stop Logan from going, to warn him that that was exactly what George Crook wanted him to do, but I didn't. All I could think of was pretty Ilse in the clutches of that misshapen savage. I dug into the sack of shells I carried in the pocket of my canvas jacket, reloaded Pa's carbine, and followed Logan out to the barn. That left poor Jack alone to explain things to the bewildered and frightened Morgenmuellers.

"Stay here," said the Indian. He slung the Henry with its fresh load over his shoulder and hoisted his saddle onto his horse's back.

"Nothing doing," I said. "I'm going with you."

He yanked the cinch tight. "You and Jack can't leave. You'll be needed here in case Rufus Brinker comes back."

"He won't. He's too badly wounded. He'll just crawl off somewhere to die, like an animal." I saddled my mustang. The little troublemaker blew out its belly when I tried to cinch up, but I gave it a kick and pulled the strap tight and buckled it before it could happen again. "I'm not doing it just to help you," I added. "I don't want anything to happen to the girl."

"Nothing will happen to her." Logan took the dun by its bridle and led it out through the barn door. I left the unbridled mustang where it was and followed him out. "He's just using her as bait," he said, mounting up. "He'll let her go as soon as he sees me."

I said, "How can you be so sure?"

He looked down at me from his superior position astride the horse. "It's my fight, Jeff. The best way you can help is to stay out of it. I'll bring Ilse back if I'm still alive to do it."

"And if you're not?"

He was silent for a moment. "She's a big girl," he said at last. "She can take care of herself until you come to get her. Either way, she'll be safe." He looked as if he were going to say something else, then seemed to think better of it and gathered up his reins. He gave the dun a kick and cantered off into the night.

Things had quieted down in the Morgenmueller household when I returned. Jack and the German farmer were standing much as they had been before, firearms in hand, but Katerina had succeeded in getting her mother into a chair and now she was dabbing a wet cloth on the spot where blood had dried into a cake on the old woman's gray hair. Frau Steiner was pale but conscious. The foreboding calm that had settled over the occupants of the room told me that Jack had explained everything.

"He's gone," I told the hider when he turned to look at me. "Headed for the mountains."

"He say anything?" asked Jack.

"He wants us to stay here."

He nodded. "I reckon we ought to respect his wishes."

"I suppose so," I agreed.

"Horses saddled?"

"Mine is," I said eagerly. "Between the two of us, we can get your mule ready to go in a couple of minutes."

"Let's go. Them mountains ain't easy to cross in the best of light." He started toward the back door.

"Take another step and I'll splatter your guts all over the room."

The toneless voice was familiar. It was one I had hoped never to hear again. Jack and I stopped and turned slowly. Bud Fowler, his broad, seamed face tight with fatigue, was standing just inside the front door, his shotgun leveled at both of us. He was wearing a knee-length yellow slicker over his dark gray suit and his black boots were coated with dust. It was obvious that he had been riding hard for some time.

"Hello, Constable," said Jack.

"Cut the small talk," snapped the other. "I been up a long

time and I'm tired and my nerves are shot. It won't take much more than a wrong look to make me pull this here trigger. Drop your guns."

We did as directed. Our rifles hit the floor with a double thud. Only then did Fowler step farther into the room. "You gents near lost me when you cut from the road," he said, stopping a few yards away. "Lucky I decided to double back and check." He glanced at me. "I'm obliged to you, son, for dropping your hat when you went down that there bank. Beats reading signs all to hell."

Fouled up again! I cursed myself inwardly.

"What is the meaning of this?" boomed Morgenmueller. He had traded his look of concern for a pompous expression. In a pinch, he turned out to be as good an actor as Jack and Logan. "I demand to know what is happening!"

"Who are you?" asked the constable in a bored tone. His eyes flickered over the antiquated scattergun in the German's hands.

The farmer told him. "What right have you to burst into a man's house and threaten his guests?" he countered.

"This right." Fowler flipped open his coat to show off his badge, then let it fall back into place. "I'm an officer of the law and these here are my prisoners. You'd be smart to stand aside, else I'll arrest you for interfering with the course of justice and for harboring a pair of wanted fugitives. What's it gonna be?" He spoke tonelessly. It was a speech he had delivered many times before.

Morgenmueller said nothing. The lawman reached behind him underneath his slicker and drew forth a pair of manacles linked together by a short length of steel chain. "Turn around and put your hands behind your back," he told Jack.

"What about me?" I asked belligerently.

"I got a pair for you, too." He snapped the cuffs onto Jack's wrists with the speedy efficiency of long practice and stepped back. "Sweeney!"

A moment later the big deputy whom I had last seen talking to Otis Ledbetter in the constable's office came in through the back door. He was carrying a bolt-action rifle with a long barrel; it may have been a Mauser, but in those days I was not enough of an expert to know for sure. One of his home-made cigarettes dangled from the corner of his mouth unlit. His eyes passed rapidly over all the occupants of the room, noted the entrances and exits and the steep staircase leading up to the second floor, and finally settled on his superior. "Yeah, Bud?"

"Cuff him." Fowler inclined his head toward me. The deputy pulled a pair of manacles similar to the ones Jack was wearing from his hip pocket and approached me with his rifle thrust beneath his right arm. He gestured for me to turn around.

"Where's the rest of your posse, Constable?" asked Jack while the cold metal was enclosing my wrists behind my back. The cuffs snapped home with a single click.

"Sent most of them home this morning," said Fowler. "Otis took off after your injun friend. He was pulling out just as we come in."

I started, rattling the chain that linked my hands together. Now Logan was in twice as much danger as he had been.

Jack said, "You boys are making a big mistake. There's a little girl up in them mountains with a killer. You'll be leaving her at his mercy if you take the injun afore he can get to her."

"Mister, I don't know what you're talking about." The lawman had his eyes open for possible tricks. "But even if I did, it wouldn't make no difference, 'cause it ain't none of my business. So let's make ourselves comfortable while we got the chance. We got a long ride ahead of us when Otis gets back." So saying, he sank down onto the sagging sofa, dusty slicker and all, and threw his shotgun across his knees. He fixed us with his commanding eyes. "Sit down."

"I would rather they remained standing, Mr. Officer of the Law." Eric Morgenmueller's voice was guttural. Standing behind him, he pressed the muzzle of his fowling piece against the back of the constable's head.

"Papa! *Was machst du?*" Katerina rose from her kneeling position beside the chair in which her mother sat. Her expression was terrified. I sneaked a look at Frau Steiner, but I guess she didn't understand what was going on, because I thought I detected a smile on her normally stony face.

"I know what I am doing, Mama," said the farmer. Then, to Fowler: "You will please to ask your deputy to unlock the manacles of my friends."

Sweeney stood awkwardly across from the sofa, covering everyone with his rifle, not sure what to do. Fowler sat like a statue and glared straight ahead at the wall.

"I knowed I should of took that there piece away from you the first minute I seen it," he said. His hands clenched and unclenched the shotgun lying across his lap.

"Regrets are not actions, Mr. Officer of the Law. The manacles." The muzzle pressed tighter.

Sweeney's eyes sought those of his superior. "Bud?"

"Don't do it," said the constable. He bit off his words.

"Do not be foolish." A note of desperation crept into the German's ponderous accent. "I do not wish to—what is the colorful phrase?—decorate the room with your brains."

"He's bluffing." Fowler glared at his deputy as if willing him to shoot.

"I do not know this word, 'bluffing,'" said Morgenmueller. "But if it means that you are betting that I will not do what I say, then the stakes, they are very high, are they not? Perhaps too high."

These words were directed at Sweeney. All eyes were on him now. He shifted his gaze about the room, squirmed beneath his superior's scrutiny. Finally his shoulders sagged. He lowered his rifle and dug a thumb and forefinger into the pocket of his vest for the key to the handcuffs.

"You blamed idiot!" Fowler shook with rage.

"Sorry, Bud." The big deputy undid my manacles, then inserted the key into Jack's.

"I know, I know," I said, before Jack could speak. "'Get their guns.'" I collected the firearms from Sweeney and then from the constable. Fowler was no more anxious to give up his shotgun now than he had been in Reuben, but eventually he let go. I stood back with a weapon in each hand and turned the show over to my partner.

Jack rubbed his wrists to force the circulation back into them. "I'd be obliged, Constable, if you stood up." He spoke matter-of-factly and without malice. The lawman got to his feet. His eyes looked as deadly as the barrels of his shotgun when he was standing behind it. "Stand next to your deputy," Jack directed. "Boy, keep them covered."

When the two officers were close together, he told them to put their hands up and patted them all over. They were carrying no other weapons. From Fowler's vest pocket he took the key to his cuffs and thrust it into his own side pocket. Then Jack made them put their hands behind their backs and manacled them so that the chain of Sweeney's cuffs passed inside the chain of the constable's. "Now sit down," he said.

The only way they could do so comfortably was to sit on the sofa with their backs toward each other and one leg stretched out before them on the cushions. All the time they were settling themselves, Fowler cursed a blue streak at Jack and Morgenmueller and each of their ancestors as far back as Adam. Nobody paid him much attention. Jack bent and scooped my Winchester and his Sharps from the floor.

"Eric, I reckon you'll keep an eye on these two while we're gone," he said to the German.

"But I am going with you," he protested.

"Won't work." Jack tossed the carbine to me and I caught it in my arms. I had already placed the lawmen's guns on the table in the dining area. "You'll only slow us up. Besides, you can't expect your wife and mother-in-law to guard these laws alone."

"Why not? They are securely shackled."

Jack regarded Fowler, glaring up at him from his awkward position on the sofa. "I wouldn't be too sure about that," he said. "Let's go, boy."

I nodded to the Morgenmuellers, cast a final glance at the two trussed-up lawmen, and went out on Jack's heels. I could still hear the constable cursing as the door closed behind me.

Five minutes later we were sitting on leather and galloping through the darkness in the direction of the mountains. The little burro, bored with its hours of inactivity, had brayed pit-

ifully when we left without it, but we had no use for a pack
animal on this trip. It was the fastest we had moved since our
escape from Reuben. This time, however, we were not running away from trouble, but toward it. The moon flashed like
streaks of lightning through the branches of the tall trees as
we left the level ground and started the long climb upward.
Only then did we slow down to look for signs of Logan's passage.

The alluvial soil on the western face of Mount Jefferson
gave us what we wanted. Jack was puzzled about the freshly
shod look of the hoofprints in the bright moonlight until I told
him that Logan had spent part of the evening paring away the
extra growth. After that his confidence didn't lag as we followed the trail deeper into the range. But there was another
set of prints as well. These, larger, uneven where the hoofs
had grown over the shoes since they had last been changed,
overlapped and obliterated Logan's clearer trail. He was
being followed, and it didn't take much thought to figure out
who was doing the following. Otis Ledbetter was earning his
salary tonight.

"The injun's a good tracker," Jack pointed out once.
"There's a third trail here, fainter than either of these others.
The injun law's leading him in deep."

For the next two hours we followed the tracks through the
mountains; at times, when the trail passed over rock or into
the shadows where it was impossible to see, we went ahead
by dead reckoning. But always Jack's instincts led us back to
where the tracks showed up again. At the end of those two
hours we came to a halt at the top of a steep rise and Jack
spent some moments gazing back the way we had come.

"What is it?" I asked.

"Take a look." He pointed a long arm over the rugged countryside.

I scanned the ghostly scene for a long time without seeing
anything of interest. Then the bottom dropped out of my in-
sides. In a patch of moonlight showing beyond the belt of
trees at the base of the mountain, a patch in which the grass
itself was tinted a ghastly silver, I spotted two men on horse-

back racing in our direction. They were going so fast that within the space of a heartbeat they were out of sight, swallowed up in the great forest of pines that resembled a ragged strip of black felt against the moon-washed background of the flat country.

"Do you think it's Fowler and Sweeney?" My voice was hushed. I didn't want to hear the answer.

"Don't reckon it can be anyone else," said Jack.

"How could they get loose? We left them trussed up like a pair of Christmas turkeys!"

"Reckon one of them had a extra key to them cuffs."

"But you searched them!"

"That don't mean it wasn't there." He swung his mule back onto the trail. "They're still a good two hours behind," he said, urging the big animal forward. "A lot can happen in two hours."

I stayed where I was for another moment. *Men chasing men chasing a man chasing a man chasing a man,* I thought. It would have been laughable if it weren't so serious. I turned and cantered to catch up with Jack.

"Sergeant I knowed got hisself killed when I was at Fort Dodge," he was saying when I got there. "Searched a renegade Shoshone afore he went to put him in the stockade. Injun stabbed him to death with a knife he had hid in his hair. Pays to be careful."

Some parts of the Cascade Mountain Range are straight up and down and completely impassable. Others are kind of sawtooth-shaped, each tooth a little steeper than the one before it, and impassable to all but fools and madmen. The part we were attempting to cross falls into the second category, and if the seven men who were following each other across that treacherous country were not what you would call fools or madmen, then you must have another name for us that means the same thing. At the end of the third hour I reined in near a thick stand of poplars and asked Jack if he had any idea where we were.

He nodded. Despite the chill of the mountain air at night, the moonlight glittered on a drop of sweat snaking down his cheek from under his hat. "This is where we first seen them paw prints this afternoon," he said.

I stared at him, wondering if the strenuous ride had shaken his brains loose. And then I heard it. A steady roar, muffled but unmistakable. The roar of water pouring from rock to rock. Without my knowing it, we had made almost a complete circle since leaving the Morgenmueller homestead, and now we were less than an hour's ride from Shoshone Falls. "Why?" I asked. "What good's it do George Crook to lead us back to where we started?"

"He's trying to throw everybody but the injun off of his trail," said Jack. "Or maybe he's just having fun. Can't go on much longer, though; his horse is slowing down." He started forward again.

Dawn was a pale promise over the mountains to the east when we came within sight of the tree-lined lake with its towering source of water sparkling in the moonlight. By night the surface of the lake was gun-barrel black. A single streak of reflected moonlight slashed white across its middle; aside from that, it was hard to distinguish the flat body of water from the hulking black shapes of the trees that crowded its shores. The ceaseless gush of the falls provided the only sound.

I saw it first. I was running my eyes over the spectacular scenery, trying to figure out where we could go from there, when I spotted a bit of movement two thirds of the way up the fluted rock wall at the top of which the falls began its six-hundred-foot drop to the inlet below. I called Jack's attention to it. We dismounted to get a better look.

For fifteen minutes we watched the lighter splash of color against the gray of the granite as it crawled diagonally up the wall. Only then, when the first fingers of light fumbled their way over the jagged horizon, did we recognize the figure as Logan's. He had his rifle slung over his shoulder and was using his hands to steady himself against the craggy stone as he followed a narrow ledge that curved its way to the top of the wall. At its end, about six feet from the summit, a shallow cave worn by a million years of wind and rain yawned a sullen invitation to all those hearty enough to try to reach it. It was obvious that this was Logan's destination. I cupped my hands around my mouth and prepared to shout at him.

A vise closed around my left arm and I gasped. I looked at Jack. He was gripping my arm in one knobby fist, but he was staring at a point below and behind the Indian. I followed his gaze. Despite Jack's precautions, the sight that awaited me there brought a strangled cry from my throat.

To the right of the falls, where the ledge began its downward swing toward the shore of the lake four hundred feet below, George Crook stood with his Winchester carbine in one hand and his free arm around Ilse Morgenmueller. With a length of rope he had tied her hands behind her back and hobbled her ankles so that she could barely move. She teetered on the edge of the shelf. The only thing that kept her from tumbling into the boiling grotto at the foot of the falls was the Indian's muscular forearm thrust across her throat. He kept the rifle steady by balancing it along his right arm with the barrel resting on a jagged feature of the wall. He had chosen the spot well.

Logan remained unaware of his danger. The roar of the falls was such that my cry was drowned out almost before it had cleared my lips. Thus unalerted, the Indian continued to inch his way along the wall long seconds after his pursuer appeared at his back. George Crook was prolonging the moment. Even from this distance, I could imagine his twisted grin as he sighted down the barrel of the Winchester and prepared to fire.

But he wasn't the only one who was getting set to kill. Jack released my arm and brought the heavy Sharps up to his shoulder, bringing the muzzle into line with the figure to the right of the waterfall. He set the trigger with a click. I braced myself for the report.

"Drop it!"

I guess I knew right away that the voice belonged to Bud Fowler. It didn't make much difference, though, because in the next instant George Crook's rifle went off and Logan was as dead as the rock wall he was climbing.

CHAPTER 14

So maybe he wasn't dead. Maybe all that happened was that Logan turned to see who was behind him just as George Crook fired, and the bullet struck him in the shoulder and sent his Henry spinning into the lake. But it all happened so fast that it looked as if Logan had been killed. The shrill scream that escaped Ilse's lips at the moment of impact didn't make things seem any less confusing either.

I don't know if Bud Fowler knew about the scene that was taking place across the lake when he arrived on foot with Sweeney behind him. At any rate, when the shot rang out he went into a crouch and wheeled in that direction, shotgun clapped to his hip. Everyone froze. For a full ten seconds the water spilling down from the top of the wall was the only thing moving. Logan, his left hand clutching his right arm where the blood was beginning to spread, stared at the man who had shot him. George Crook faced him in silence, grinning, I suppose, like a hyena. Ilse wobbled precariously on the narrow ledge. Jack, Fowler, and Sweeney kept their guns trained on the Indian policeman, who was unaware of their presence. And I just watched and waited for all hell to break loose.

But it didn't. At least, not right away. Logan remembered the revolver in his holster and went for it, but pulled up short when the other Indian swung the Winchester one-handed by its lever, jacked a fresh shell into the chamber, and pulled down on him again in the time it took him to get his hand from his injured arm to the butt of the Colt. "Go ahead!" George Crook shouted over the roar of the falls. "It'll look good on my record!"

Logan said nothing. He stood with his hand poised halfway to the belt gun and didn't move another inch.

"You disappoint me, Logan!" said the other. "I thought you had more guts than that!" He was trying to goad him into going for the gun. It didn't work. "All right!" The policeman's grin vanished. "If you won't use it, get rid of it. Drop it in the lake."

Logan said, "Why should I? You'll kill me anyway."

"Drop it, goddamnit!" George Crook tightened the armlock he had across the girl's throat and dangled her feet over the edge. She squealed in terror. "It's a long way down, Logan! You'll have plenty of time to think about your mistake before she hits them rocks!"

I clenched my fists. If I'd had the chance right then, I would have finished the job on the Indian lawman's face.

Logan hesitated a beat. His pursuer let Ilse slip six inches. Finally he reached for the gun and lifted it gingerly out of its holster. The tiny splash it made when it hit the lake sent ripples all the way across the surface.

"That's better," said the other. He set the girl back on her feet.

"Now's your chance!" I told Jack. "Shoot him!"

"I wouldn't do that." Fowler had turned away from the drama on the cliff and now he and his deputy had their firearms trained once again on Jack.

I stared at him, scarcely believing what was happening. "Constable, that man on the cliff is a murderer! He killed a man in Idaho and he's about to do it again!"

Fowler was unconcerned. "If he's George Crook, he's a lawman. Anyhow, it ain't none of my business."

I swung back to Jack. He had the rifle braced against his shoulder and his cheek pressed against the stock. I said, "What are you waiting for? Why don't you shoot?"

"I reckon I can't." He lowered the rifle.

"Now you're getting smart," said the constable.

"Why can't you!" I was beginning to wonder if I were the only sane man on this side of the lake.

"He's too far away and too close to the girl. I might hit her."

George Crook's taunting voice floated down from the high ledge. "I was beginning to think you weren't coming," he shouted to Logan. His finger was on the trigger of his rifle and he was in complete control of the situation. "I got bored. Thought I might have to pass the time by reading." He looked at Ilse. "Or something."

"I didn't have much choice after you issued that challenge," said the other Indian.

"You're a fool, Logan! A fool for coming here and a fool for climbing up there when you thought I was hiding in that cave. And now you're a dead fool." He leveled the carbine along the rock and took aim at Logan's chest.

"Don't do it, injun!"

The shout, gruff, threatening, echoed around the lake. George Crook snapped his head to his left. The rest of us followed his gaze. On the south shore of the lake, seated solidly astride a huge Appaloosa, fat old Otis Ledbetter held a rifle pointed upward at the Indian policeman. I only caught a glimpse of him, however, because out of the corner of my eye I spotted a movement high above the old deputy's head and looked up to see none other than Rufus Brinker scuttling along the top of the rock wall. He swayed a little from the loss of blood he had suffered since leaving the Morgenmuellers', but it didn't seem to slow him down any as he made for the summit. I remembered Jack's words: *Mad or sane, all animals head for higher ground.* He must have been hiding there all this time, and been flushed out by the loud voices. I seemed to be the only one who had noticed him.

"Otis, get away from there!" Fowler shouted to his deputy. "He's law!" This time the Indian policeman's face turned quickly in our direction. It was his first intimation that he had not been alone with Ilse and Logan from the start.

Otis didn't budge. "Law or no law, he ain't got no right to commit murder. Drop the gun, mister!"

It looked as if George Crook were going to obey. Slowly he lowered the Winchester from its position atop the rock. Then he wheeled and fired. The deputy's rifle went off at almost the same instant, but the bullet went wide as Otis arched his back and tumbled out of the saddle. His horse screamed, reared, and took off through the trees at a gallop, leaving its master lying in a heap on the shore of the lake with one arm in the water.

Fowler let out a bellow of grief and rage and fired at George Crook, but his shotgun's range was far too short. I heard the shot falling through the trees. Sweeney's rifle spoke at the same time; Mauser or not, though, it had no accuracy at that great distance. His bullet *spanged* against the rock a good twenty feet below the ledge upon which the Indian lawman stood.

The only hope was Jack's Sharps. He rasied it again but stopped short of squeezing the trigger. George Crook was holding Ilse in front of him now, and there was no way he could shoot the Indian without hitting the girl. Jack waited for his chance.

The chief of the Nez Percé police was determined not to give it to him. Still holding the girl, he returned his rifle to its former position and sighted once again on Logan, who in the confusion had managed to advance ten feet or so closer to his pursuer. He had obviously been hoping to get close enough to wrestle the gun away from him, but had been unable to do so fast enough because of his useless right arm. Now there was no way George Crook could miss. I could hear him laughing over the rumble of the falls.

Suddenly he looked up. Rufus Brinker, crouching directly above him at the top of the rock wall, had accidentally kicked some rubble loose onto the ledge and alerted the Indian to his presence. The madman was a sight to see, squatting atop that granite promontory. All those shots had whipped him into such a frenzy that he was ready to attack anything from any height, and now, sitting on his heels, arms outstretched, chains dangling from his wrists, there was little doubt but that he was about to pounce two hundred feet straight down to where George Crook stood. Scarcely had this thought occurred to me when Rufus leaped.

George Crook was already moving. He let go of Ilse to free his other hand and swung the barrel of his carbine upward to meet the threat. The girl flattened out against the wall. In that instant, Jack fired his Sharps. At the same time Rufus Brinker came down on the Indian with a kiyoodling bellow, and together he and George Crook went plummeting down into the rock-studded grotto at the base of the six-hundred-foot falls.

To this day I swear that an instant before the madman took him in his deadly embrace, George Crook lost his grip on his Winchester and fell back against the wall as if struck by a battering ram. It can only be that from a distance of over five hundred yards Jack had hit what he was aiming at. Never again would I laugh at those old-timers' boasts about the capabilities of the Big Fifty.

For a long moment after the two men disappeared from view beneath the boiling waters at the foot of the cliff, we stood watching the busy inlet. Then I remembered Ilse. She was standing where George Crook had left her, hugging the side of the cliff and afraid to move for fear of stumbling on her bonds and sharing her abductor's fate. Logan was inching toward her from the other side of the falls, but he was growing weak from loss of blood and was beginning to teeter himself. Once his foot slipped and he was forced to use both hands to catch himself. I could picture his grimace of pain as he hoisted himself back up. I left the others and hurried over to where I had left my horse.

"Where do you think you're going?" Fowler challenged. He was all lawman again, although now there was a hollowness in his curt tone that had not been there while Otis Ledbetter was alive.

"Straight up." I mounted the mustang and took off in the direction of the cliff. Fowler's shotgun remained silent.

There wasn't much use in getting down to take a closer look at Otis. As I rode by his great hulk of a body, I could see a hole the size of a twenty-dollar gold piece where George Crook's bullet had come out his back. He had been dead before he hit the ground. Fowler was right. There wasn't another officer in Reuben who could hold a candle to Otis Ledbetter when it came down to real law enforcement. Including the constable himself.

I found Logan's dun tethered to a stunted yellow pine growing out of a crevice in the rock wall. George Crook's paint was grazing nearby, much as it probably had been when the other Indian had come through, leading him to believe that Sam Dailey's killer was up on the cliff. I left my horse there and headed on up the steep slope. Before long it narrowed into the ledge that had led Logan into a trap and the Indian policeman to his fate. This was a shelf of rounded rock some eighteen inches wide at its broadest point, but which grew so narrow in some places that it was hard to tell it from the numerous other crags in the weatherworn cliff. I wondered how the Indian had ever managed to get himself and Ilse to the spot where he had called Logan out. What was more important, I wondered how I was going to get both of us back.

I looked down just once while I was making my way toward the splash of color that was the Morgenmuellers' only daughter—and immediately resolved not to do so again. What I saw was a dizzying view of the two hundred-foot tall pines that crowded against the gray wall *from the top,* and, beyond them, of the water tossing and swirling angrily over the jagged rocks in the grotto at the bottom of the falls. Below me the cliff fell away for nearly one hundred and fifty yards until it disappeared into the thick growth of trees. The waterfall was a roaring in my ears as I inched along the scantiest portion of the ledge, chest pressed against the stone, hands grasping the wall's gnarled surface. My nostrils filled with the sharp smell of granite dust. Twice I had to fight back a sneeze for fear that it might make me lose my footing.

Ilse stood with her back to the wall on one of the more roomy sections of the uneven shelf. Even so, her inability to stretch out her arms because of the bonds that held them behind her back made her position extremely dangerous; it had the effect of pulling her forward toward the edge so that she swayed back and forth, her heels teetering on the slippery stone. Her skirt was dusty and ragged at the hem, her blouse wilted. One of her blonde braids had come unpinned and now dangled loose over her left shoulder. Her face glistened with perspiration. Beyond her, Logan had passed beneath the arch of the falls and was dragging himself toward her at a painful pace. His right sleeve, hanging useless at his side, was drenched with blood. It was obvious that George Crook's bullet had shattered the bone. He used his left hand to grasp the crags in the fluted rock and pull himself forward. Because of his weakness, he was forced to stop and rest after each effort, and it was for this reason that I got to the girl first, even though he had been working toward her for the past forty-five minutes. No sooner had I reached Ilse than she fell against me in a kind of swoon. From then on I was supporting both of us.

"Give me your knife!" I shouted to Logan over the din of the falls when at last he had joined us. He shook his head weakly and motioned for me to turn her around. All this time he was smiling that funny half-smile that had infuriated me on so many occasions.

I did as he directed, and in the space of a few seconds he had sawed through the stout ropes on Ilse's wrists and ankles. He nearly lost his balance straightening back up, but caught himself just short of pitching headlong over the side. In so doing he lost his knife.

"Damn!" I heard him say, as he watched the glittering shard of steel tumble into the white water. "There goes my last defense!"

I won't bore you with the details of how we got back. It's enough to say that, inching our way along that treacherous ledge with Ilse Morgenmueller spread-eagled between us, we found the going twice as hard as it had been on the way in. At one point Ilse's foot slipped on the eroded rock and Logan lost his grip on her arm. For several seconds she dangled, afraid to breathe, while I dug my fingers into the rock and held on to her wrist for dear life. Then I pressed my shoulder against the cliff and freed my other arm to haul her back up onto the shelf. My hands were sweating. She started to slip and I felt rather than heard her breath catch in her throat. I tightened my grip. I wondered fearfully if her weight might pull her arm out of its socket. That danger was prevented when she managed to get hold of my left wrist with her other hand. I dug in my heels and tugged until Logan was able to curl his good arm around her waist and, fighting to hold on to his own precarious balance, set her back onto her feet. Her breath came out in a gasp of relief. Fifteen minutes later we were back on solid ground and walking single-file down the slope that led to the shore of the lake.

Logan fought me when I tried to help him into his saddle. "Go help an old lady across the street," he growled. Grasping the saddle horn in his left hand, he went to swing himself up onto the dun's back, fell back, and tried again. That time he made it. I pretended not to notice how pale he had become as I helped Ilse onto the front of my own saddle and mounted behind her.

Jack and the two lawmen were waiting for us when we got to where Otis Ledbetter had fallen. They had turned the dead deputy onto his back and now Fowler and Sweeney were looking down at him sadly, hats in hand. Jack alone looked up as we approached. His nod when he saw me was almost imperceptible.

"I can't figure why he done it," the constable was saying. "Weren't none of his business nohow."

Jack eyed Fowler with the air of a doctor observing the symptoms of his patient's illness. "Constable," he said flatly, "if you ain't got it figured out by now, you ain't going to."

"What's that supposed to mean?" Fowler challenged, fixing the other with his lawman's glare.

Jack didn't bother to answer. He slipped his Sharps into his saddle scabbard and mounted his mule, which until now had been grazing with the officers' horses among the pine needles that covered the ground.

"Hold it, mister." The constable raised his shotgun to cover the hider. "You ain't going nowhere. You're under arrest. You, the boy, and the injun."

"What for?" Jack's tone was bored.

"What you think? For murder."

"Who'd we kill?"

Fowler smirked beneath his handlebar moustache. "You ain't so dumb, mister," he said approvingly. "But save that stuff for the jury. There's a dead injun down by Quartz Mountain that might not believe you're so ignorant."

"Who says we killed this here injun?" asked Jack. He placed his hands on his saddle horn and looked as if he really wanted to hear the answer.

"Why," began the lawman, then stopped. He glanced involuntarily in the direction of the raging falls. "George Crook," he said at last.

Jack waited for him to go on.

"I know what you're thinking. But I got it in writing. You forgot all about that little telegram the injun sent from Oakland, didn't you? The one where he says you killed his partner." There was a gloating expression on the constable's face.

"I reckon you got us, then," shrugged Jack. Fowler grinned. "That's a heavy piece of evidence, a wire that names us as killers."

The grin faded. "Well, your names ain't exactly in it," he said slowly.

"They ain't?" The man seated astride the mule looked surprised. "Then how'd you know we was the ones done it?"

"By the description. What else? A man with a mule and a burro, a kid, and an injun. That fits you."

"Description like that could fit a lot of people I know. But I reckon it was enough to get a warrant."

"You know damn well there ain't no warrant," snarled the other. He was losing and he knew it.

"No warrant?" asked Jack.

"There wasn't time."

My partner held up his hand in a farewell salute. "So long, Bud," he said. He swung his mule westward.

"Hold it!" said Fowler. "You don't think I'm gonna let you go just like that!"

"Way I see it, Constable," said Jack, sauntering away along the lake shore, "you got no choice."

Reuben's chief peace officer spluttered and fumed and blew out his moustaches.

"Want me to stop him, Bud?" Sweeney unslung his long-barreled rifle and stood with it cradled in his hands.

"Oh, shut up."

I left them with Otis Ledbetter's body and caught up with Jack. Ilse and I made quite a load for the little mustang, but it bore us with little complaint. I have to admit that I was getting used to the little troublemaker by now. "I wish there were something we could do for Otis," I said to Jack.

"Ain't nothing nobody can do for him now," he replied.

"He turned out to be quite a man."

"I expect he always was." Jack watched the trail ahead. "Reckon I know who it was killed them two outlaws down in Juárez."

Ilse, riding sidesaddle in front of me, opened her eyes and looked around. She had been asleep since I'd put her there and this was the first time she'd stirred.

"How are you feeling?" I asked her gently.

"Sleepy." I could barely hear her. "I want to go home."

I was about to tell her that's where we were going when I heard a groan near me and turned just in time to see Logan fall out of his saddle and crumple into a heap on the ground.

"Jack!" I exclaimed, and started to dismount. But he was already off his mule and kneeling beside the Indian and he motioned for me to stay where I was. Swiftly he pulled his kerchief from around his neck and tied it as tight as he could around the upper portion of Logan's arm above the wound. He thrust the handle of his skinning knife into the knot and twisted it inside the makeshift tourniquet until the flesh bulged.

"Get a doctor," he said. "Hurry! Leave the girl here."

I hesitated, looking at Ilse. She was wide awake now. "He is right," she said, and slid down to the ground before I could stop her. "You will find Doctor Richter four houses north of my home on the west side of the road. I will be all right here."

It took all of Jack's strength to hold the tourniquet in place. "Get going, Jeff! He ain't got much time."

I broke into a gallop then, and I was halfway back to the settlement before I realized that he had called me Jeff.

CHAPTER 15

I practically had to kidnap Dr. Richter to get him out to where Logan lay near death. A middle-aged man with a long, sober face and sidewhiskers that connected with his moustache, he was just getting ready to go out on his rounds when I came upon him climbing into his buggy. He didn't understand a word of English; in order to get my point across I was forced to act out what had happened to the Indian and point frantically in the direction of the mountains to the east. Even then he was reluctant. Maybe he thought I was some new kind of outlaw who was trying to lure him into the woods where the rest of my band was waiting to rob him of his purse and carriage. Finally he nodded and motioned me forward while he followed.

We met Eric Morgenmueller at the end of the driveway. The farmer was in his hunting clothes and seated astride the bare back of a muscular workhorse. He had seen me going past his place, he explained, and quite naturally wanted to know what had happened to his daughter. I hardly need add that he was in a highly nervous state. When I assured him that Ilse was all right and that the doctor was for Logan, he asked how he could help, and I told him that we might need his buckboard to get the Indian back to the settlement. He quickly agreed and withdrew to hitch it up.

Richter's buggy was still bouncing when he scrambled down with his black bag in hand and hurried over to examine the wounded man. Jack or Ilse had torn away the bloody sleeve and one of them, probably the girl, had filled Jack's canvas bucket with water from the lake and used it and a scrap of material from her skirt to cleanse the arm of blood. Logan lay with his head propped up on a bed of leaves and pine needles. His face was so ashen that for a moment I was afraid we had come too late. I watched him for several moments before I could make out the slight rise and fall of his chest, and even then I wasn't sure if I were really seeing it or if it was just my imagination. The hand Jack was using to hold onto the tourniquet was red with blood—his own, for he was grasping the skinning knife's razor-edged blade in his fist. But he refused to let go as the doctor took out a large bottle of something (hydrogen peroxide?) and finished cleansing the wound.

It was an ugly sight, a ragged mass of blood and meat and bone splinters with here and there a scrap of cloth from where the bullet had passed through Logan's shirt. Richter barked something to Ilse in German, whereupon she got up from her kneeling position beside the Indian and trotted off toward the wooded section near the lake. While she was gone, the doctor splashed alcohol onto a gauze pad, applied it to the wound, and wound a cotton bandage tightly around it.

"What happened to the lawmen?" I asked Jack during the operation.

"Lit out," he said. He switched hands on the tourniquet and wiped the blood off on his shirt. No sooner had he done so than the cut hand began to bleed again. "Throwed Ledbetter over George Crook's saddle and headed south. Reckon they'll hire a wagon in Cascadia to take the body the rest of the way back to Reuben."

"Fowler didn't offer to help?"

He shook his head. "Weren't none of his business."

Ilse returned, carrying two stout pine boughs which she had broken off the trees. Each one was about two feet long. Richter placed the sticks on either side of Logan's wounded arm and bound them in place with bandages from shoulder to wrist. All the time he babbled away in his native tongue while the girl translated.

"Dr. Richter wishes to transport him to his office, where he will remove the bone chips and attempt to reset the arm," she told us. Her face was pale but composed. "It is possible that he will have to amputate." She paused. "He also says that by applying the tourniquet, Mr. Butterworth may have saved Mr. Sleeping Bow's life."

As if by an act of Providence, Eric Morgenmueller chose that moment to arrive with his buckboard. His wife was with him. Seeing Ilse, she gave a little squeal of mixed relief and joy and hopped off to take her in her arms.

"*Geht's gut*, Mama," the girl asserted, but still her mother smothered her against her breast and murmured what sounded like a string of prayers in German. Ilse told her something in which I recognized my name and Jack's.

When she was finished, Katerina left her and came over to take me in an embrace nearly as energetic as the one she had given her daughter. Over her shoulder I saw the girl smiling at me shyly. She had a smudge of dirt on her cheek that made her look much younger than she was.

Jack was next to receive Mrs. Morgenmueller's gratitude, but by that time he, Richter, and the farmer had succeeded in laying Logan on the blankets spread out in the bed of the wagon, and he was too busy watching the Indian for any sign of change to pay much attention to her words of thanks.

The doctor climbed into the buckboard beside Logan and removed the tourniquet from around his arm. "*Schnell!*" he shouted to Morgenmueller in the driver's seat, and Katerina and Ilse barely had time to get on before the farmer gave the reins a snap and the two-horse team leaped forward with a clatter of hoofs and a jolting and squeaking of springs.

"Follow!" called Ilse, just before they rattled out of sight around the base of the mountain.

I looked to Jack for confirmation. He was already in the saddle and gazing down at me, his kerchief-turned-tourniquet now serving as a bandage around his right hand. "I reckon you heard her," he said, and struck out in the wagon's rutted path.

I tied the mustang to the back of the doctor's buggy, which everyone appeared to have forgotten, and drove the rig back.

The doctor's office took up two of the three rooms in his house, one of which, lined with German medical books and reeking of alcohol and various medicines, was used for consultation while the other answered for an operating room. Richter slept in the third. The Morgenmuellers were all seated on a wooden bench in the consulting room when we got there. Ilse slept with her mother's arm around her shoulder. Eric told us that the doctor was at work on Logan in the next room, and Jack and I took seats in the two captain's chairs near the door. He was asleep in less than a minute.

Not me. Despite my sleepless night, my mind was too full of the events of the past twenty-four hours for me to feel the least bit tired. I said once before that the smell of the plant Logan called yarrow put me in mind of a doctor's office; that works both ways. The minute I had stepped into the consulting room with its hodgepodge of pungent odors, I was catapulted back to a long-unused cornfield north of the Umpqua River, where I had seen a fugitive from an Idaho Indian reservation crush a strange herb into a green paste and apply it gently to the injured thigh of my pa's bay. Now I sat here waiting while another practiced a similar brand of magic on the fugitive himself. Life is strange.

When the operating room door finally opened, I had watched the hour hand creep twice around the dial of the big clock that stood between two rows of medical journals atop the bookcase opposite me. I looked from it to the drawn, moist face of the doctor. Everyone in the room was awake now, and all eyes were on him.

He delivered his message slowly, with frequent pauses in between words, and with an awful sinking sensation I thought, *Logan's dead*. But when I looked to the Morgenmuellers to confirm my fears, I saw that their faces were alight.

"He says," translated Ilse, whose expression hardly fit the

care with which she spoke, "that the Indian is going to be all right."

Everyone looked at me. I suppose they were waiting for me to say something, but I'm afraid I disappointed them. I fell asleep.

I slept most of the day. I have a dim recollection of someone shaking me awake, and of stumbling down the road to the German farmer's house, but that's all I can remember until the moment I came awake and found myself lying in bed staring up at the rafters in a sloping roof. Sunlight slanted in through a window next to the bed. Not being sure where I was, however, I had no way of knowing if it was coming in from the east or from the west. Had I been asleep for twenty-four hours?

"About time you stirred." It was a familiar voice, dry and caked with dust. A lot of years have passed since I last heard it, but I'd recognize it now. I sat up.

Jack, looking as tall and as rail-thin as he had the first time I'd seen him, stood just inside the doorway. He had his campaign hat pulled low over his eyes and his Sharps in his hand. "We got four good hours of daylight left," he said. "Let's ride."

Mr. and Mr. Morgenmueller were waiting at the bottom of the stairs when we got there. The living room had been restored to its former neat appearance since the night before. Frau Steiner, a bandage affixed to the side of her head (we had thrown a lot of business Dr. Richter's way), smiled and nodded at us from her place in one of the upholstered chairs. Her attention was centered on Jack.

"I'm sorry we got to leave you holding the bag like this," Jack told the Morgenmuellers. "I reckon you'll be hearing from the authorities in Idaho afore long."

Eric shook his massive head like a bull besieged by flies. "I fear they will learn little from me. My English, it is not so good yet." His blue eyes twinkled.

The farmer's wife must have noticed me looking around,

because her eyes sought mine and she smiled. "She is in the barn."

I came upon Ilse speaking German to the white-faced milk cow in soothing tones. In the sunlight coming in through the window in the loft, her hair matched the hay that was heaped everywhere. She didn't look up as I approached.

"Where's Herman?" I asked her.

"He is repairing the corncrib." She stroked the cow's nose. The animal watched me indifferently, its jaws working from side to side at a mouthful of hay.

"Your mother said you wanted to see me."

She nodded. "I wanted to thank you for saving my life."

Summoning all my courage, I said, "The best way you can do that is to give me permission to visit you from time to time. I live quite a ways south, but—"

"I cannot do that." She kept her attention on the cow.

I guess I looked pretty silly standing there with my mouth open. I closed it.

"Please don't be angry," she said. "It is Papa's wish that I marry Karl Richter, the doctor's son. I cannot see anyone else."

"I see," I said, but I didn't. "Do you like him?"

"He is very nice."

"That isn't what I asked."

"Yes, I like him."

"Enough to marry him?"

She didn't answer for almost a minute. "It doesn't matter," she said at last. "It has already been decided."

"Where is this Karl Richter now?" I bit off my words.

"Away at school. When he comes home we will be married."

"And when is that?"

"Next spring."

"You can't get out of it?"

She shook her head. "It is Papa's wish. I cannot disobey."

I took a deep breath and let it out slowly. With it went my

anger. I felt empty. "Well, good luck," I said, and turned to
go.

"Jeff!"

I turned back. She went up on tiptoe and kissed me on the
cheek. "*Danke*," she said.

Our mounts were saddled and waiting for us in front of the
farmhouse. Jack shook hands with Eric before climbing up
onto his mule. "Reckon we'll say our good-byes here," he told
the farmer. "We'll stop by and visit the injun, but then we got
to be going."

"The settlement is owing you a hundred dollars for the mad
dog. Where shall we send it?" Morgenmueller shielded his
eyes from the declining sun to look up at him.

Jack said, "Keep it. You're going to earn it when you talk to
the law. I ain't got no address anyway."

The little burro brayed impatiently at the end of its halter.
I mounted the eager mustang, and, after accepting a wax-
paper-wrapped package of duck sandwiches from Mrs. Morgenmueller ("It will put good German meat on your bones"),
we said our good-byes and left.

"What was that about them keeping the money?" I asked
Jack after we had passed out of earshot. "How are you planning to operate without cash?"

"What makes you think I ain't got cash?" he encountered.

"But, you said—"

"What's that look like?" Out of his back pocket he hauled a
roll of dirty bills big enough to choke—well, a buffalo. I decided not to press the point.

The sunlight glittered on a tiny gold chain hanging down
from his left saddlebag. "What's that?" I said.

"What's what?"

"That." I leaned over and seized the chain in my fist before
he could stop me. Pulling it out, I saw that a locket of some
kind dangled from the other end.

"It's just a good luck piece," he said, and made a grab for it,
but by that time I already had it open. The portrait inside was
that of an attractive woman with dark hair and a strong chin.

It had to be at least thirty years old, but it didn't take much imagination to figure out what the woman looked like now. I laughed.

"Gretchen Steiner! I knew she was sweet on you from the start."

He snatched the piece of jewelry out of my hand and stuffed it back into his saddlebag. "Belonged to her dead husband," he growled, eyes glued on the road ahead. "She give it to me to say thanks for helping bring her granddaughter back safe and sound. That's all."

"If you say so," I replied, with a straight face. Ilse was already a dim memory.

Logan was sitting up in the bed Dr. Richter kept for his convalescent patients when we got to the operating room. His injured arm, newly splinted and swathed in fresh bandages, lay on top of the blanket. "About time you got here!" he snapped at us before we had even set foot inside the room. "I might as well be talking to myself as to this butcher who calls himself a doctor." He indicated the sober-faced physician taking his pulse beside the bed. Richter ignored him.

A rare grin flickered over Jack's countenance. For the second time since I had known him, I saw the flash of gold teeth he usually kept hidden as if afraid somebody might try to steal them. "Glad to see you're better," he said. He tossed the package the farmer's wife had given us onto the Indian's stomach.

"At last!" said Logan, tearing off the wrapping and sinking his teeth into the first sandwich. "This quack's been starving me."

I've often wondered if Dr. Richter might have understood a little English, or if he'd just picked up the drift of his patient's speech by the tone of his words. At any rate, it was with exaggerated grace that he snapped shut the face of his watch, bowed to the Indian, and departed. Jack chuckled.

"He's just doing his job, you know," he said. "Ain't no need to act like a heathen injun."

Logan finished his sandwich in silence.

"How's the arm?" asked Jack.

The Indian shrugged his good shoulder. "It's still there. I doubt that I'll ever get much use out of it, but it's better than an empty sleeve." He looked at Jack. "That was some shooting." It was the closest he came to thanking him for saving his life. But it was enough.

Jack said, "Weren't much to it. With the Big Fifty, all you got to do is point it and fire. If anyone deserves a compliment, it's Rufus Brinker. I wouldn't make a jump like that to save my own mother. Even if I had one."

There was a little silence. I broke it. "How long are you going to be laid up here?" I asked Logan.

"Not more than a couple of days, if I can help it," he replied. "I've a hunch there'll be a circular with my name on it waiting on Bud Fowler's desk when he gets back to Reuben, and I'd rather not be around after that. Besides, I have a new wife to get back to."

"Reckon it's safe?" asked Jack.

"My first stop will be at the army post to turn myself in. I'm sure the tribe will speak for me, once they hear George Crook's dead." He wrapped up the remainder of the sandwiches and put them on the instrument stand next to the bed. "The Nez Percé police are due for a flushing out."

"What happens then?" I inquired.

Logan said, "I'm thinking of California. I've had enough of life on the reservation, and my wife has relatives there. After that . . ." He shrugged again. "But that's in the future. I'll be in Idaho for some time yet, so I'd appreciate it if you'd drop me a card to let me know how the hunt comes out."

"Under which name?" Jack regarded him with a faint smile.

The Indian looked at him, and presently he smiled too. "Try Sleeping Bow," he said.

Jack offered his right hand and Logan—or Sleeping Bow— took it in his left. "It's been interesting," said the hider.

Logan laughed. "You ought to have been on this end." Then he looked at me. "Stay off those cliffs, okay?"

I flashed him a grin. "Okay."

Back on the road, I asked Jack which way we were going. His gaze swept the mountains to the east.

"By now he's circled the settlement and come back to the trail. Reckon we'll just keep going the way we are and pick up his tracks on the other side."

That wasn't as easy as it sounded. The road had been built right on top of the old buffalo trail, and its surface was so hard an elephant carrying a full load of rocks on its back could have stomped right down the middle without leaving so much as the outline of a footprint to mark its passing. But that didn't slow us down. Several times Jack dismounted, spent some time wandering head-down around the road's grassy bank, then, his confidence recharged by something he had seen, swung up onto his mule's back with a new energy and push on. I don't know what he saw when he made these stops, and I didn't ask. I could tell he wasn't in an explaining mood.

Afternoon bled into evening, and we were still moving. The idea never occurred to me to suggest making camp. Even without the threat of George Crook behind us, the hunt retained an air of excitement, something like a throbbing heartbeat that grew louder and louder with each step we took. I could feel, deep within me, that we were nearing our quarry. I think this feeling emanated from Jack. Rock-steady as ever on the outside, he must have been ready to bust apart from within. To ask him to stop when he was so close would be nothing less than a crime.

At length, though, we did stop. The sun was only a memory in the blue-black of the night when we fixed a starvation meal and climbed into our bedrolls thirty yards from the road. We were up again in less than five hours, and I got the idea as I stumbled through the motions of breaking camp that the only reason we had stopped at all was to give our mounts a rest. Since yesterday's trek had not been a particularly hard one, that meant rough going up ahead. It was still dark when we pulled out.

Those next few hours seemed to flit by like telegraph poles at a fast gallop. Jack said little, perhaps preferring to save his energy for the hunt. He was on his mule most of the time, stopping only to squat on the ground (the road dead-ended fifty miles north of Mount Jefferson) to check some tiny sign in the rock-hard earth. As always, he saw tracks I didn't, smelled scents I couldn't. The mule flared its nostrils frequently when it was moving, drawing in and puffing out hot air like a bull in rut. It seemed that it, too, had caught the scent, and with it recaptured the spirit of its youth when buffalo ruled the plains. As for me, I was swept along like a leaf in a twister. I could not have freed myself even if I had wanted to, things were happening that fast.

An hour before noon, in a region full of humpbacked hills west of the Hood River, we came to a full stop at the top of a mound covered with timothy and wild wheat. I was about to ask why we had halted when Jack cut me off with a slashing movement of his left hand. He seemed to be listening. I followed his lead.

The air seemed silent at first. But after we had sat still a few seconds, I became aware of the life that throbbed all around us. A slight breeze rustled in the nearby treetops and skimmed through the grass at our mounts' feet. Somewhere close, a small creature thumped along the ground unseen. Above us, a handful of small birds climbed and swooped busily, calling to each other in distinctly nonmusical squawks and peeps. Other than that I could detect nothing that would claim my partner's interest. "What is it?" I asked, my voice scarcely above a whisper.

"Birds," said Jack. "Hear them?"

I listened to the birds' abrasive barking for another moment. "Starlings," I said.

He nodded. "Starlings, but more than that. Buffalo birds."

When I didn't comment, he went on. "Buffalo hide's full of ticks. Them's what the birds live on. They used to follow the herds by the thousands in the old days. You could hear them squawking from here to Texas."

My heart was thumping against my chest. "Does that mean we're there?"

The wide hat brim twitched in a manner of curt decision. "Near."

We sat quietly for a moment. I guess maybe we were both a little awe-struck at the idea that we had come to the end of the hunt.

"Ride like hell!" The shout exploded from Jack like a case of dynamite in a house afire. His mule shot forward. He was halfway up the slope of the next hill before I could collect enough of myself to follow, and then I slapped the startled little mustang on the rump with a blow that would have killed a snake. My teeth snapped together with the jolt and we galloped off in Jack's dusty path.

We topped that hill, followed it into a hollow, and clattered up the next. We didn't have roller coasters in those days, but if we had, the swelling, undulating sensation this caused would have reminded me of one. After we had gone over three or four of these low swells, the ground flattened out, leaving only one long, gently graded slope up ahead. It was crowned at the top by a huge spreading oak. I remember this last detail especially well because I saw Jack standing in its shade as I came over the top of the last hill. Away over his head, the noisy birds that had inspired our haste were circling and playing tag with each other in the clear blue sky. The racket they made was deafening, or at least it seemed so under those circumstances. Jack's mule stood motionless beside him.

I came to a skidding stop at the top of the grade and bounded off in the same motion. When I joined him, Jack had already slid his Sharps from its scabbard and was stretched out on his stomach on the ground, sighting down the barrel at something in the lush green valley below. "Look at him, boy," he said, and his voice sounded funny, like I'd never heard it before. "Ain't he a sight to see?"

I got down beside him and looked in the direction his rifle was pointing. At first I didn't see much of anything. It was a pleasant place, full of tall grass of one shade of green and bushes of another, with here and there a tall elm or a grove of poplars to break up the monotony. A creek meandered more or less through the middle of the scene—a tributary, I imagine, of the mighty Columbia. I wondered with a shrinking sensation in my chest if three years of expectation were making Jack see something that wasn't there.

And then I saw it too.

It had come out from behind a tangle of blackberry bushes, where it had most likely been drinking from the creek. Big, dark as walnut stain, it started out huge in the bearded head and shoulders and great bulging hump, then tapered back to a rump almost as narrow as my own. The black horns that curved out and around from its wooly pompadour were a perfect match. As it walked, it twitched its tail at the cloud of flies that surrounded it and tossed its mammoth head as if spoiling for a fight, or, the next best thing, a cow in heat. Its chest was deep and its hocks were shaggy. It was indeed a sight to see. It would have been the chief of its herd had it not been the last buffalo in the United States.

"As good-looking a animal as I ever did see," Jack was saying. He set the Sharps' action with a click of the rear trigger. "Better. Killed me a old bull big as that south of the Platte in Nebraska, but that was at the end of the shedding season and its coat wasn't near so full. Yes, sir. This one's worth three years."

He fell silent as he drew a bead on the monstrous bull. I waited for the report. In my mind's eye the beast was already hit, folding to the ground like Pa's old corncrib had done in the big wind of '93. To my surprise, I didn't feel elated. I had been anticipating this moment ever since Jack had agreed to take me along, looking forward to it as one of the high points in my life. But it didn't feel so high. I realized then that this was the same feeling I'd had when George Crook had Logan trapped above Shoshone Falls and Jack told me he didn't dare shoot for fear of hitting Ilse. I felt sick and helpless. I didn't close my eyes, but I cringed in expectation of the big gun's roar.

And then a funny thing happened.

There are moments in your life that stand out so clear in your memory that years later you begin to wonder if they really happened, or if you wanted them to happen so badly that you fool yourself into thinking that they did. This was one of those moments. I was lying there on my stomach feeling sorry for that old bull, and mad at myself for feeling that way, and Jack was bearing down on him with that Sharps that never missed, and I was waiting for the report and for the bull to go down like a sack of potatoes, and then it looked like the barrel of the Sharps moved to the left ever so slightly and fire leaped from the end of it and roared and the buffalo jerked up its head and turned tail and galloped out of sight over the next hill, its tail twitching, before Jack could reload.

There was a long pause while the thunder of the report echoed away into the distance and Jack lay there with a fresh cartridge in the chamber and nothing to shoot at.

"I missed, goddamnit," he said at last, but he didn't sound as disappointed as he should have.

CHAPTER 16

I never found out for sure if Jack missed that shot on purpose or by accident. It's hard to believe that a man who could hit his target dead on from a distance of over five hundred yards one day could completely blow a shot at another from less than two hundred the next. In any case, I like to think that at the last second it occurred to him how wrong it would be to pick off the last living remnant of the life he knew best, and that he did move his rifle just enough so that it fired two feet to the animal's left. If he did, though, I doubt that he would have admitted it to himself, just as he hadn't after he'd missed a similar shot two months before he met me.

Jack and I parted company that day. I didn't explain why I was leaving, and he never asked. He didn't even seem surprised. Deep down I guess he knew the reason. I took enough of the supplies to get me back to Citadel, but when I offered to pay him for them, he told me to get the hell out of there.

I swung up onto the mustang's back and looked down at him from the saddle. He had extracted his bore mop and can of gun oil from his saddlebags and was unloading his Sharps prior to cleaning it. He treated that gun like a sick baby. "Where do you go from here?" I asked him.

"East a ways." He saturated the wad of blackened cotton at the end of the wooden rod with the yellow oil and thrust it down inside the barrel. "Buffalo ain't about to cross the Columbia here because it's too wide, and there's too many towns over to the west. I'll catch him up in the mountains."

"Where then?" There was no need to speculate on whether his aim would improve between here and the mountains.

"Reckon I'll head over to Portland. Friend of mine used to run a shop there that sold fifty-caliber ammunition. Hope he's still around."

I guess I should have stopped there, but I just couldn't let it go. "And then?"

He looked up from the rifle between his knees, squinting at me in the bright sunlight. "Boy," he said patiently, "do I look like a fortuneteller to you?"

It was a dismissal. I said good-bye and swung the star-faced mustang south. The last glimpse I had of Jack was of an old man standing on a hilltop beside a big mule and a mangy little burro, cleaning the barrel of a Sharps buffalo rifle. His face was all but hidden beneath the downturned brim of his broad campaign hat. Just before I passed beneath the crest of the next hill, I thought I saw him raise his long right arm in a wave, but I couldn't be sure. He might have been adjusting his hat.

I stopped in Reuben on the way home to see if I could buy back Pa's bay, but the scrawny old man who ran the livery stable told me he had sold it two days before to a farmer who wanted to give his fourteen-year-old son a horse for his birthday, so I was stuck with the mustang. I didn't mind that too much, though, because by then I'd grown used to the little troublemaker and every rotten trick it pulled on me. I reckon you could get used to being punched in the mouth if that's the way you were greeted every morning before breakfast. How else can I explain the way I felt that November morning in 1905 when I shoveled a path out to the barn through three feet of snow to find the mustang dead in its stall, frozen stiff as a wooden horse on a merry-go-round?

The stable owner had some big news for me, though. Billy Granger was dead. It seems young Rick looked up from his dime novel the morning after Bud Fowler and his posse had left town to see the youthful bank robber choking at the end of his shirt, the other end of which he had braided and tied to the bars in the window of his cell. Rick rushed in and cut him down, but by that time it was too late. Two days later Billy's mother came and took his body back home for burial. It must have seemed like high time to her; as far as she was concerned, he had been dead for some time. I asked the stable owner how Fowler had reacted to the news. His unshaven face crinkled in a grotesque grin.

"Just don't get in his way when he spits," he warned me. "He'll burn a hole right through you."

Not only did I not get in the constable's way, but I made it a point to take the side streets out of town so that I didn't bump into him and give him an excuse to lock me up for assaulting an officer. That week had not been a particularly good one for Reuben's most respected citizen.

The north and south branches of the Umpqua had receded quite a bit since the rain, and I had little trouble crossing them. I got back to Citadel in plenty of time to take Theodora Corcoran to the Memorial Day dance. Soon after that, I sold the farm to a land speculator from New Rumley, Ohio, who was looking to make a killing out of what he called the "undeveloped West" and used part of the proceeds to pay Pa's debts. Next came Uncle Jake, whom I suspect was disappointed to see my debt to him resolved so easily. What was left went into the bank to gather interest while I proposed to Theodora Corcoran.

This last act came as much as a surprise to me as it did to Theodora and her mother, who had just about given up hope on me as a possible match for her daughter. Looking back on it, I guess you might see it as a logical result of my rejection by Ilse Morgenmueller, but at the time this wasn't so clear and it caused me a great deal of thought between the time of my betrothal and the informal ceremony at the Presbyterian church in August.

By that time I had made a down payment on some better farm land north of town and we moved in right away. I couldn't make a go of it, though—it takes a special breed to be able to cope with Oregon's unpredictable climate—and after eight years of pure heartbreak we picked up and moved to Kansas, where I bought a house ten miles outside of Topeka.

Life was pretty good there. Say what you like about marriages on the rebound, Theodora and I had a good one going right up until the night she died of scarlet fever in February of 1926. By then she'd presented me with three strong sons. That about ends my story, except for one last thing.

One day late in 1912, my youngest son, Ted, talked me into taking him to the movies. I remember the year because it was right after his namesake, Teddy Roosevelt, had disrupted the Republican National Convention in Houston by opposing his former Secretary of War, William Howard Taft, for the presidential nomination. I had been one of Mr. Roosevelt's staunchest supporters ever since he had collected Spain's bloody debt to the United States on San Juan Hill, and I voted for him both times he ran for president, including the time he ran at the head of his "Bull Moose" party and lost. Anyway, it took six-year-old Ted most of the day to coax me into taking him to the boxlike theater on Topeka's west side; I'd been to the movies, or flickers as we called them in those days, once before, and found them frivolous in comparison to the live plays that had once been presented in that same building. But I went again. Like the man for whom he was named, Ted could talk a rock into turning over so he could collect fishing worms from beneath it without scraping his hands. I've always thought that he could have gone into politics had he not chosen to be a better farmer than his father ever could be. Of his two brothers, Jack, the eldest, went to pharmaceutical school and opened up a drugstore in Hays, and Joseph Pulitzer migrated down to Oklahoma in 1915 to work in the oil fields. I haven't received a letter from either of them in over a year. But to get back to the theater.

The place was heated by coal, and coal must have been cheap that year because it was stifling. What was worse, every seat was taken. You haven't suffered until you've sat in a room crammed with fifty or sixty hot, sweating people and tried to keep your mind off your discomfort by looking at a jumble of yellow-tinted images fluttering across a four-by-six-foot screen erected in the front of the room. Little Ted was enjoying it, but then kids are easy to please.

It was a Western. The heroine, a girl with dark tousled hair and big eyes, was firing a rifle out the window of a log cabin at a pack of whiskey-crazed Indians galloping around on the backs of paint ponies and shouting (I assume, for there wasn't any sound) blood-curdling war cries while they poured arrows into the building from all sides. The rifle was a 1903 Springfield, which struck me as funny because modern weapons and wild Indians just didn't mix. Meanwhile, the hero, carrying a single-action Colt .45 revolver that never seemed to run out of bullets, crouched atop a rock outcropping about sixty yards from the cabin and picked off the savages one by one at rifle range. I looked around me to see if anyone else had noticed these details. No one had. Everyone else in the room watched the actions on the screen with looks on their faces as if they thought they were seeing the real thing. I turned back to the screen.

The hero had killed what he thought was the last Indian and went in to claim his quivering prize. While they were embracing, a leftover redskin crawled in through the broken window. The heroine saw him over her rescuer's shoulder and opened her mouth in a silent scream. The hero spun around. The Indian leered evilly and advanced toward him with a knife in his hand. Heroically, the hero threw aside his gun and stalked forward to meet him with nothing more than his bare hands. They closed. The Indian forced the hero into a corner. The knife, slowed by the white man's grip on the savage's wrist, descended toward the hero's chest. Again the girl screamed. Then the hero ducked, twisted the Indian's arm, and the would-be killer was flipped to the floor, where he fell upon his own knife. At last the embrace between the handsome hero and the pretty heroine was completed. The image on the screen faded. The lights came up.

I sat there for a couple of minutes afterwards, staring at the blank, fly-specked screen which a short while before had been the center of everyone's attention. The room emptied and I was still there. I ignored Ted's impatient tug on my sleeve.

I had recognized the Indian.

Of course, I could have been mistaken. The situations were so similar that I may only have thought I was seeing the same man. I told myself that, and yet I didn't believe it. For a moment, while the Indian on the screen had been stalking toward the hero, knife in hand, I saw in his leer the ghost of a faint smile I had not seen for fourteen years. At Ted's insistence, I got up and left the theater, but the image of that smiling face haunted me all the way home and lingered throughout dinner.

Just to make sure, I came back the next night without Ted. Again I saw the hero vanquish the last of the Indians he was to meet outside and bound into the cabin. Again I saw him take the frightened girl into his arms. For a second time I watched as the grinning savage climbed in through the window. This time I saw that he held the knife in his left hand, and, as he grappled with the hero, I noticed something else. I noticed that he never used his right arm. The camera took pains to hide it, but all through the fight the Indian kept his right arm stiff at his side. When he fell and squirmed in his death agonies, the limb lay motionless on the floor. It might as well have been artificial for all the use he had made of it.

There were no film credits flashed on the screen in those days, so I had no way of checking for Logan's name. I thought of writing to the company that made the film—it was one of those early southern California firms that have since passed out of sight—but I never got around to it. I remembered that Logan had told us about going to California. Maybe he had finally found his niche. I doubt it, though, because I never saw him on the screen again, playing an Indian or anything else, and after that day I was a rabid film fan. Maybe it was just a passing thing. I suppose now I'll never know.

As for Jack, I never heard from him again. I thought once or twice about trying to get in touch with him, and even wrote a letter once to a magazine that specialized in publishing notices by people looking for lost loved ones, but although they printed it I never received an answer. For all I know,

Jack may never have learned to read or write anyway. I think
it's more likely that he just didn't see it.

Maybe it's a good thing that we didn't meet after that part-
ing on the hill. Age affects different people different ways, and
I'd have hated to have to remember Jack Butterworth as a
decrepit old man in his dotage, or dead, as he must surely be
by now. I'd rather think of him as a lean old hider carrying a
Sharps Big Fifty and riding a mule on the trail of a buffalo
he'll never shoot because he knows if he shoots it, he'll die too.

And that's the story you didn't read in the papers about the
spring a youth and an old man struck out across Oregon in
search of the last buffalo in the United States.